KINGDOM OF TODAY'S DECEIT

ROYALS OF FAERY

BOOK TWO

HAYLEY OSBORN

LEXITY INK
PUBLISHING

Lexity Ink Publishing
Christchurch, New Zealand

Publisher's Note: This is a work of fiction. Names, characters, places, and incidents are a product of the author's imagination. Locales and public names are sometimes used for atmospheric purposes. Any resemblance to actual people, living or dead, or to businesses, companies, events, institutions, or locales is completely coincidental.

Book Layout ©2020 BookDesignTemplates.com
Cover Design ©2020 by Covers by Combs
Editing by Melissa A Craven

ISBN 978-0-473-55235-0 (paperback)
ISBN 978-0-473-55236-7 (ebook)

For Nicola
For always buying my books, even when you don't have to, and even when the shipping is the same price as the books.

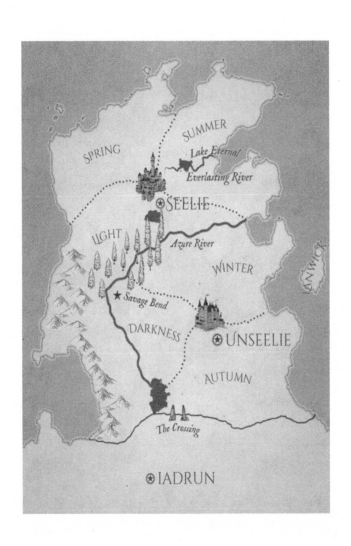

ONE

THE VIEW out my window and across the lowlands of Unseelie was the most beautiful I'd ever seen. Rolling green hills grew slowly higher, rising into snow-capped mountains in the distance, and a thick forest of pine trees stretched in the opposite direction as far as I could see. If I stood in just the right place and pushed up onto tiptoes, I could glimpse the brilliant blue waters of some far-off river.

I hated it.

That view was the only thing I'd seen in three months. That, and the inside of my rooms high in the Unseelie castle. They looked like lodgings fit for the finest guest, but the moment I opened my door to step outside or threw open a window for fresh air, it became obvious this was a cell. A spell prevented me from setting foot outside the four walls that surrounded me. I couldn't even open the window wide enough to poke my head outside.

My only pleasure—and it was a small one—was that the Unseelie King had ruined Queen Rhiannon's plans when his men attacked the convoy of Seelie soldiers as they stole me away to Seelie in the dead of night. I should be rotting in the prison beneath the Seelie Castle—or, more likely, dead. Instead, I was languishing in a locked guest room, complete with an enormous bed with more pillows than one person needed, a luxurious bathing room, views to die for and the added bonus of three large gauges in the stone walls.

I imagined myself to be the only dot of light in the king's life, too. By capturing me, he'd unknow-ingly gained a bargaining chip with the Queen of Seelie. Although she'd failed to take me hostage that night, she had captured his two children—Crown Prince Fergus Blackwood and his sister, Princess Willow.

In the beginning, the king had come to my room daily. During those visits, he tried to swap information with me, offering me small details about Mother; that she appeared to have escaped that night, that no one had seen her since, that he

thought she was alive and well, hidden away somewhere. In exchange for those pitiful tidbits, he'd
expected me to answer questions about his children and what Rhiannon wanted from them.
When I couldn't, he'd come at me with snarling
demands and threatening magic to pry what I
knew of Rhiannon's plan from my lips. He hadn't
needed to use magic. I'd have willingly told him
everything, had I known.

After that first week, once he realized I had
nothing to share, he stopped visiting, leaving me
totally alone. I hadn't seen or spoken to another
person in weeks. I only had myself and that
horribly beautiful view for company.

Today though, something felt different.

More than once this morning, I heard footsteps
outside my rooms, but when I threw open my
door, there was no one around.

I couldn't be certain, but there seemed to be
movement down in the stables. Apart from the
smallest corner, the stables were out of my view,
but it seemed as if there were more people than
usual moving around down there.

Sick of waiting for whatever was happening to
walk into view, I cracked the window open and
pushed my nose into the small gap, inhaling the
sweet spring air and listening in case there was
talk below about what was happening.

Had the king retrieved his children? Had he somehow kept me out of the bargain? I hoped so. I missed Fergus more than I imagined I would. I'd cried many tears locked up in here alone, imagining how Queen Rhiannon was treating him.

A knock on my door made me jump and whack my head on the window frame. No one ever knocked at my door. Food arrived on the little table in the far corner by magic, three times a day—leftovers disappeared the same way. And when the king had visited in those early days, he'd thrown the door open without warning, usually so hard it banged against the wall behind it.

"Come in," I called, rubbing my head.

The door opened slowly to reveal a fae wearing a long black cloak, hood pulled high to hide his face. "Come with me." His head moved as he cast his eyes over the flouncy teal dress I'd chosen to wear today. Not so long ago, my best friend and I would spend hours admiring the beautiful fae dresses that hung in her mother's wardrobe. Now that dressing myself in the over-the-top gowns that hung in my cupboard was the only way to occupy my day, I'd be happy never to see another of these stunning dresses again.

Finishing his appraisal of my attire, the man added, "And wear your riding pants."

"Where are we going?" I remained where I stood beside the window, weighing the safety in complying with or disregarding his wishes. I was tempted to conform just to get out of this room, but I didn't wish to walk headlong to my death. The only reason I could come up with as to why the king had kept me here so long was because he truly believed he could swap me for his children. If that was the case, if this man intended to take me to Seelie, I was as good as dead. Rhiannon wouldn't make the same mistake with me twice.

"It is of no concern to you." The fae stepped out into the corridor as if he expected I would magic myself into the clothes he desired me to wear and follow that second.

He seemed unaware that my magic—wayward at the best of times—was impossible to control when locked in a room with iron woven into the walls, ceiling and floor. The three large gauges that decorated the walls were my doing, as was a long-since-fixed cracked window. All because I'd tried to use my magic to break the windows and escape during those first weeks. Using it in front of a stranger to undress was asking for trouble. "It is if you want me to go with you."

He spun around, his black cloak flaring out behind him.

I folded my arms over my chest. Once, the arrogant tilt of his head and just knowing he was fae would have been enough to make me hide beneath the bed. Now I wasn't half as scared as I probably should have been.

He gave the sigh of the severely inconvenienced. "We are going to see Fer—the Crown Prince."

My heart leapt at the sound of Fergus' name. And at something else, too. I took a single step forward. "Where is he?" I didn't care about the reply. I just wanted to hear that voice again.

"I'm sure you're very well aware of the answer to that question."

I smiled and took another step forward, dropping my voice to a whisper. "Jax?" Now I was listening properly, I was certain the fae standing in front of me covered head to toe in the shadows of his cloak was Fergus' best friend. Surely he was the only one so familiar with both of us that he would almost use Fergus' first name when speaking with me.

The man stiffened. He shook his head, then beckoned me to follow him.

I folded my arms over my chest. I wasn't going anywhere until he showed me his face. And until he'd given me a chance to change clothing like a normal person. "No."

The fae stopped, his back to me.

"Come on, Jax. I thought we were friends. Show me your face and talk to me like you usually do."

The fae moved so fast, I didn't realize he had until we were both inside my room with the door slamming in his wake. "My identity is to remain a secret." He spoke through his teeth.

Those few words told me far more than I'd asked; the man in front of me was Jax, and because nothing happened around here without the king's approval, the king had commanded Jax not to show his face when speaking with me. "What King Aengus doesn't know won't hurt him. I take it you haven't come to rescue me?" I hadn't heard from Jax in all the months since I arrived at the Unseelie Castle. The last time I saw him, he was waving goodbye from the back of his horse, not long before the rest of us were captured. I assumed he'd gone back to Fergus' island, but perhaps he'd been in Unseelie all this time.

He ripped the hood from his head, his brown eyes fiery—a perfect match for the color of his hair today, which was orange. He seemed broader than when I had last seen him, but that could have been my imagination. Under the heavy cloak he wore, it was difficult to tell. "Of course not," he spat. "My loyalty is and always has been to Unseelie. And to the Crown Prince."

I lifted my eyebrows at the intensity in his voice. "You're angry with me?" I wasn't sure what I'd done to receive such a harsh tone. The last time we'd seen each other, we'd been friends.

"Get changed." His voice was brisk. He turned his back, clearly having realized the reason I hadn't waved my hand and done as he demanded.

"What is it I've done to offend you while locked in this room these last three months, Jax?" He was silent, so I threw out some options, my anger at his silent accusation growing. "Do you think I'm working with the Queen? Perhaps you think I let the king lock me up in a small room for months on end so Queen Rhiannon could do what she desires to your prince?" I held back the words that wanted to follow. The words that would remind Jax I was bonded to that prince, that magic had chosen the two of us to spend the rest of our lives together. I held them back because even though the part of me that was ruled by the spell wanted those words to spill from my mouth, the rest of me didn't want that bond any more than I wanted to be trapped here in Unseelie.

He turned around, his finger jabbing into my chest. "That's exactly why I'm upset. You're here.

They're not. You might have the king fooled, but I know you had something to do with their capture."

He ... *knew?* "Based on what evidence?"

His stare grew pointed. He didn't have to speak for me to understand. The evidence was as he'd said. I was here and Fergus was in Seelie.

Officially, I was from the Seelie Kingdom, but I had no allegiance to Queen Rhiannon. I had no allegiance to either of the fae kingdoms. If I had my wish, I'd forget all about Faery and return to Iadrun, where I'd lived my entire life until a few months ago. "Did you forget she tried to kidnap me, too?" The same night she took them, her guards had taken me.

His eyes narrowed. "How convenient she split you away from them." His body hummed with anger. "Seems like her plan was to take you somewhere else." In the gaping silence that followed, I could almost hear him say *somewhere other than the Seelie prison.*

"She captured me while I was still in Unseelie. Fergus and Willow were already in Iadrun." I sighed. I could see why he would have problems believing me. Mostly, I imagined, it was the fact that Queen Rhiannon was also my aunt. For the last three months, every single day I went over the details of that night, wondering how everything happened as it had. I could only come up with one reason she'd kept Fergus and me apart, but it was a good one. "Maybe the Queen wanted to keep our magic separated?"

Jax was silent. He must have considered that, too.

If Queen Rhiannon was aware of our bond, she also knew we were stronger as a team. Perhaps she thought our power together might rival hers. "I want Fergus back as much as you do." My voice softened. So much happened the last night Fergus and I saw each other. In the short time we'd had to discuss it all, we decided to ignore our bond and remain on opposite sides of the Faery/Iadrun border. Since then, I'd had plenty of time to think it all through, and I still wanted to ignore the bond. But damned if I wanted anyone to lock Fergus up and throw away the key.

Jax watched me for a long moment and his eyes softened. "Good. Get changed. We're going to get him."

My heart leapt. "Are you serious?" I raced for my wardrobe before he could answer, pulling out a pair of black riding pants, a black scooped-neck shirt and knee-high riding boots.

As I threw my clothing onto the bed, Jax turned his back again. "We need to be at the Border Bridge by dusk tomorrow."

I had limited knowledge of the landscape of Faery. I knew Unseelie occupied most of the land closest to the border with Iadrun, and that Seelie had a narrow strip on the western side of southern Faery, which opened out into a much wider parcel of land in the north. "How long will it take to get there?" The last time I went to Seelie, we hadn't crossed a bridge. We'd flown on the horses of the Wild Hunt.

His loud sigh told me any self-respecting fae should know the answer to that question, but he answered anyway. "A full day on horseback. Perhaps longer."

I stripped off my dress and pulled on my pants while Jax kept his back to me. "Don't you think we should have left sooner, perhaps?" That was a tight timeframe. We might need to travel into the night.

"Given you'll be walking, I imagine we probably should have left last week." Jax's voice was hard, and with his back to me, I couldn't tell if he was joking.

I pulled on my shirt, feeling more like myself than I had in months, and took a final look around the room. There was nothing here I wanted to take with me. "Walking? Why?"

Jax glanced over his shoulder, checking I was ready before turning around. "Hold out your hands."

I did as he asked and, using a spell so he didn't have to touch them, he slapped a set of iron cuffs around my wrists. The metal burned where it touched my skin and I hissed. "What the heck, Jax? Take them off." The iron against my skin sizzled and burned, lighting a fire in my wrists all the way down to the bone.

Jax took my cloak from the closet and fastened it around my neck. Pulling his own hood up, he opened the door. "I'm sorry, Bria. I can't do that."

I glared at his back. "Then I'm not going with you." What was the point if I was still a prisoner?

He rounded on me. "Think about it, Princess." He spat the word at me, his body so tense it looked like he might explode. "You are a prisoner of the king. How else am I to take you from this castle?"

I looked at my feet. He was right. A prisoner couldn't just walk out of the castle. I pulled the long sleeves of my shirt beneath the cuffs to dull the burning, though it made little difference, and lifted my chin. This was to get Fergus back. For that, I would wear cuffs for the next two weeks if I had to. "Let's go, then."

Jax wasn't joking when he said I was walking. He tied a long rope to the center of the cuffs, running it back to the belt on his pants. He sat bareback on Flame—his chestnut horse—and walked her at what, for me, was a slow run.

Flame's hooves clopped against the cobbled street that took us from the stables to outside the castle walls. I gritted my teeth as we left the castle grounds, curious fae stopping their work to watch as we passed by. As the homes around the castle became rolling meadows and the cobbled streets gave way to dirt roads, I waited for Jax to stop and let me on his horse. Or at least slow down.

After months of being stuck indoors, I was unfit, my muscles weak. Running stole my breath and my legs and ankles ached with every step. Not to mention, it was near on impossible to run properly with my hands locked together. What was the point in changing into riding gear if he expected me to run all the way to Seelie? "Jax," I puffed. "I need a break."

He pulled back his hood and turned to watch me without slowing his horse. "You look fine to me."

"I'm ... not." I could barely form the words over my heavy breathing. My chest ached and my sides burned, and if he didn't stop soon, I might collapse on the ground.

He shrugged and turned back to survey the landscape in front of him. In the distance to our left was a line of willows, and I assumed, behind them, the river. Straight ahead and to our right was a thick stand of forest, huge white flowers hanging from the branches. There was beauty everywhere I looked. If only I had enough energy to take it in.

Instead, it was taking all my energy not to turn an ankle on the deep ruts that littered the road as I waited for Jax's answer. Something felt, not wrong exactly, but off. "We are going to get Fergus, aren't we?"

In a single movement, he pulled his horse to a stop and turned to face me. The moment I could stop running, I collapsed onto the dirt road on my back. "Of course." Strands of his shoulder length hair floated around his face. He pushed them away with the back of his hand and glanced past me in the direction we'd come from.

Still struggling to catch my breath, I followed his gaze. The Unseelie castle was some way behind us, but because of the rolling hills and the dip we'd stopped in, only the ramparts were currently visible. There wasn't another soul in sight. I pushed onto my elbows. "I can't run all the way to the border." At the moment, I didn't think I could get off the ground if I tried.

A canteen of icy cold water—condensation dripping down the sides—appeared on the ground in front of me. I tipped some over my head, then finished the rest without stopping to breathe.

"We have to be careful." Jax's eyes remained on the road behind us.

I placed the lid on the canteen. "There's no one around." The road was empty. As it had been since we left the castle.

"Just because you can't see danger, doesn't mean there are no threats."

This was Faery, after all. I knew next to nothing about the dangers here, other than that there were many.

Jax turned to look in the other direction and sighed. "I can't let you on the horse yet. It's not safe. But I will slow my pace as much as I can, and once we reach the trail beside the river, you can ride with me." He gave his hand a flick. "And that should help." Light green magic pooled around him before flowing toward me and dissipating.

"What was that?" With any luck, it was a spell to give me more energy.

He clicked his tongue, and his horse's ears twitched. "A double step spell. Each step will take you twice as far. Let's go."

I pushed to my feet. Might as well get this over with. I walked past Jax and up the road. As I walked, the rope between us pulled taut. I turned to find that in a few steps, I'd used the entire length. This, I could deal with. "What are you scared of?" I asked as Jax gave another look over his shoulder.

He shrugged. "All the things that might hurt us."

Obviously. But I didn't know what they were. "Like...?"

Jax pulled up beside me, walking Flame slow enough for me to keep up. "This road..." He nodded to the dirt road in front of us. "Did you wonder why we've seen no one travelling it?"

"I guess..." I hadn't. I'd been too busy trying to catch my breath.

"The road marks the border between the Winter Court and the Court of Darkness." His raised eyebrows suggested that should be all he needed to say. It explained the white on the trees I'd seen earlier. I thought it was flowers, but now I looked closer, I could see snow covered the branches and the ground near the forest.

But it explained nothing else. "And no one's allowed to use it?" That would certainly justify the state of disrepair the road was in. I'd been dodging huge ruts from carriage wheels all day.

"You walk this road at your risk. Especially if you're not a fae of the court through which you're travelling."

A shiver went up my spine. I couldn't even imagine what happened out here that gave the road such a reputation, and I didn't want to find out. "So why don't we take a different route?"

"This route will get us to the Border Bridge the fastest. If we're set upon by fae from the Winter Court, we'll move into the Court of Darkness. In theory, they may not cross the border outside their lands, so we should be safe."

In theory. I wasn't sure I wanted to put that into practice given there was nothing stopping anyone stepping from one court and into another. "And if the Court of Darkness come after us, we'll go into the Winter Court."

Jax nodded.

"But aren't both courts part of the Unseelie Kingdom?"

Jax nodded again. "That doesn't make them friends."

Clearly. "Hopefully they don't come for us at the same time." Or at all. I glanced over my shoulder, now as nervous as Jax looked. "

"It wouldn't be the first time." He nodded out across the Court of Darkness lands to where the willows marked the river. "A little farther upstream at Savage Bend, King Aengus has some of his army protecting the narrowest part of the river from Seelie." Everything on the other side of the river was Seelie territory, everything this side was Unseelie. My knowledge of Faery was limited, but that was something he didn't have to tell me. "You might not see them at the moment, but there are plenty around who might want to hurt us just for the fun of it." He shrugged. "Or because we'd make a tasty meal."

"And you don't have any allegiances you can call on? Any fae you know from either of these Courts? Family?"

"I have no family but Fergus." His eyes darted out toward the river on our left. "And even if I did, I'm from the Autumn Court, which is in the opposite direction and no help while we're out here." He clicked his tongue and Flame started trotting, leaving me to break into a jog to keep up. "Once we reach the river, we have to travel through Winter Court lands. We'll be in the forest by then."

"Which makes us safer?"

Jax shrugged. "Who can say?"

And who-knew-what would be hiding for us there. "Can't the king protect us?" He was in charge of Unseelie, and we were going to get his son back.

"He can. And he does. Officially, the Lord of the Winter Court doesn't condone attacks, especially on those who work for the king. Unofficially, and until the fae that make the attacks get caught, he allows them to do as they wish."

We continued in silence after that as I dropped back to run behind Flame. The rolling hills soon made way for thin forest, and once we entered that, the sound of rushing water lingered in the air.

As promised, Jax stopped his horse and untied the rope between us. He magicked up another canteen of water, which he passed to me as he gave a long, low whistle.

I gulped the water down so tired I could barely move. I wanted nothing more but to lay my head down and close my eyes, but I couldn't see that happening soon. At the sound of movement behind me, I jumped, imagining Winter Court fae approaching with bared teeth.

But it wasn't fae who'd found us. It was someone better. "Raven!" The horse from the Wild Hunt that Fergus had loaned me stood on the trail. She nickered and came closer. I buried my face in her neck, breathing in the hay and stables on her skin. She smelled so good.

The last time I'd seen her was when Fergus and I left her and Obsidian glamoured in the Unseelie stables. For three months I'd wondered if she was okay, if anyone other than the stable hand knew she was there. I should have known Jax would look after her. "I can ride her?" I was so excited that my voice shook. Seeing Raven was a close second to seeing Fergus again.

He nodded. "On the ground only. Don't want to draw attention to ourselves."

I didn't care if I rode her on the ground or in the air, as long as I didn't have to run anymore.

I held my cuffed hands out. "Can you remove these now?"

He shifted on the back of his horse, his gaze falling to the ground.

"Jax? Riding will be easier if I'm not cuffed."

"It might be easier without them, but you can still do it cuffed." He made a clicking sound with his tongue and Flame moved off.

I watched his back, unease growing in my belly. Three months ago, I counted Jax as a friend, now I was wondering if I'd read him wrong. "This isn't a rescue, is it?" I pulled myself onto Raven's back. There was no way I wanted to walk again, and with what I was about to accuse him of, there was a high chance he'd take Raven away from me.

He turned Flame in a circle until he was looking at me. "What else would it be?"

I shrugged, my heart racing. Jax was Fergus' best friend. What I was about to suggest was outrageous. Or would have been if I was Unseelie, too. "An exchange."

Jax scoffed. "A what?" With a click of his tongue he turned Flame away, and they started back along the trail.

Raven and I followed. He hadn't denied it. Or offered any other explanation. I drew in my breath and spat the words out. "So, you're not planning to swap me for Fergus?"

Jax laughed. I wanted it to sound hard and mean, but it was jovial, as if I'd told a joke and not at all like I'd accused him of doing something so horrible. "Really, Bria? Do you know what Fergus would do to me if I had him released by giving you over to Queen Rhiannon?"

I imagined Fergus wouldn't be happy, though it didn't escape my attention that Jax hadn't answered the question. I shook my head. "You're right. Sorry. I've spent so much time alone lately that I've started seeing everyone as the enemy. Even when I shouldn't."

He smiled over his shoulder, and it seemed genuine. Perhaps I really was seeing things that weren't there.

"Apology accepted. There is a chance we could run into someone who might report back to the king, albeit a slim one, but I have to leave the cuffs on you in case we do. You have to look like my prisoner."

The cynical part of me said the other purpose of the iron cuffs was for tamping down my magic, which, if he did plan to swap me for Fergus, would be useful—there was no way the Queen would want to give us the chance of combining our magic and overpowering her. The rest of me decided there was no reason not to trust Jax. "The king knows you've taken me from the castle?" He must. It wasn't like Jax had tried to hide me as we left.

"He does." He said the words slowly and cleared his throat. "I talked him into letting you out of your room by suggesting we agree to the queen's terms and swap you for Fergus and Willow." He shook his head, eyes sincere as he caught my gaze. "But I never intended to do it. I just needed to get you out of that castle."

My shoulders relaxed. He had a plan. "Well, thanks. I needed to get out of that room."

The trail followed the path of the Azure River, sometimes so close, Raven could bend her neck and drink from the brilliant blue water right off the trail, but mostly I could only hear it behind a thick wall of evergreen trees. As soon as we entered the woods, the temperature dropped and grew cooler with each step the horses took. The farther we traveled from the Court of Shadows, the more snow lay on the ground—I hated to imagine how thick it might be in the center of the Winter Court lands. Sparkling icicles hung from slowly waving tree branches, sometimes tinkling against each other like wind chimes, other times dropping and sinking into the hard ground like knives slicing through butter. Just one more thing that might kill me if I wasn't careful.

Jax slowed his horse, waiting for me to stop beside him. The light was just beginning to fade from the day. "We'll stay here for the night."

Here was the forest trail and with the river on one side and a thick stand of pine trees on the other, there was no way to get off it. Certainly not while riding the horses. Probably not while walking, either. "Um..." I didn't know what constituted a good place to stop in Faery, but I was pretty sure this wasn't it.

Jax laughed and waved his hand, light green magic flowing from it. The pines parted, pulling back to reveal a cottage that belonged in a children's story book. The roof was red and the walls white, and as I watched, the arched door swung open, inviting us to follow the winding path across the snow-covered lawn and inside. A little stone well with a matching red roof stood on one side of the cottage, and a two-bay stable—the feedboxes already filled to overflowing with hay—stood on the other.

"What is this place?" I whispered. "It's beautiful."

Jax smiled. "One of the king's private cottages—he has lodgings in all three of the Unseelie territories. This one is on loan to us tonight while we work to bring his son home." He slid off his horse and grinned up at me. "We're perfectly safe here. The place is impenetrable."

It seemed as if we were the only ones around. The snow on the path and front lawn was pristine and untouched, and although the door had opened and there was food in the stables, I imagined magic was responsible. I followed his lead, climbing from Raven and walking her toward the stables. "Shouldn't we keep riding?" Darkness was coming, but he'd said we would have to push hard to reach the Border Bridge in time. He hadn't yet shared his plan to bring Fergus home, and I suddenly wanted him to. "What will we do tomorrow?"

Jax turned, walking backwards. Strands of fiery orange hair swirled around his face in the light breeze. "We'll leave before dawn and fly the horses to the Border Bridge."

"But you said—"

"We can't fly the horses during the day, but we'll get away with it before dawn. No one will think twice if they see the Wild Hunt out at that time of day."

That was likely true, but something about his planning and excuses sounded ... hollow. In my head, I heard how stupid I was being, but I couldn't stop asking questions of Fergus' best friend. "Then what?"

"Then we wait at the bridge for the Queen to arrive with Willow and Fergus. As they're crossing the bridge, I'll take out one pillar below, they'll fall into the water, and we'll take the horses downstream to rescue them."

That seemed rather risky. "What if their hands are tied, and they can't swim properly? Or what if they get hit by falling debris on the way into the water and get knocked out? What if the water is so cold they can't survive?" There were so many *what ifs* to this plan.

Jax's forehead creased as if he didn't understand the questions. "They both have powerful magic. They'll be able to keep themselves afloat and out of danger."

Something wasn't adding up. I'd seen Fergus in the hours after his last escape from Queen Rhiannon, when I'd had to wrench two magic suppressors from his back, and I'd seen what using his magic straight after removing those suppressors did to him. So had Jax. Fergus had nearly died that time. The same would happen if Fergus used his magic straight away again. I couldn't believe Jax was suggesting it. I didn't voice these thoughts. Instead, I asked something else that was bothering me. "Why you? Why did the king choose you to do this?" And why only him?

Jax settled Flame into her stall and turned to me, eyebrows raised. "Apart from the fact that I've been Ferg's best friend since we were babies?"

I wasn't sure being friends with the prince counted as a reason the king would choose him for this rescue. Not when I knew Jax had very little combative magic. Under attack, he only had enough magic to have one shot at using it should something go wrong. Why didn't the king send someone else along with better combative magic to help him? Or use someone else completely?

Jax sighed when I didn't speak, spelling out the answer I hadn't reached. "Because I have certain skills that make me indispensable in times like this."

Jax was a puka and therefore could shapeshift—it was in that magic that his abilities were strongest, according to Fergus. It was a skill he kept quiet, and even the king wasn't aware exactly how good he was at it. "How does that make you indispensable?"

He took Raven's reins and directed her into the other stall. "Puka have a natural immunity to glamour. Should the Queen try to trick us tomorrow by glamouring someone else as Ferg or Willow, I'll be able to see right through it."

Okay. That was a solid reason for sending him. A weight lifted from around my heart with his words. There was no reason to mistrust Jax. There never had been.

Once he'd settled Raven in for the night, he put a hand on my shoulder. "I understand this is strange for you, Bria, but you mean a lot to Fergus, which means you also mean a lot to me. I'm trying to help you, okay?"

I nodded. I was being stupid. It was like I'd told Jax before. All that time spent on my own had affected my judgement.

He looked at my cuffs. "Let's get those off you." With a flick of his wrist, the cuffs sprang open and fell into the dusting of snow at my feet.

"Thank you." My wrists were thick bands of weeping skin where the cuffs had been. I didn't like my chances of finding something cooling like aloe in this winter landscape. Actually, I didn't like my chances of Jax allowing me to head out into the forest and look for anything that might help them heal. Not while we were in the lands of the Winter Court. And not when nightfall was so near.

With his hand on the small of my back, he guided me toward the house. "The king has special crisped potatoes on the menu at the cottage. It's the only place in all of Faery they're served. Smell that?" He sniffed the air.

I followed his lead to be greeted with the inviting, if somewhat unhealthy, aroma of potatoes and duck fat. "They do smell good." My stomach growled. After a day of running, I was sure the aroma of any hot food would have the same affect.

"And the beds are the most comfortable you'll ever lie upon."

My bed in the Unseelie castle had been the same. "I am feeling tired," I heard myself say. Sleep would do me good. I was seeing Jax as the enemy he wasn't. In the morning, I'd realize my concerns were nothing but the worries of an idle mind.

The arched door to the cottage yawned in front of me, the scent of waiting food drawing me forward.

"I knew you'd do the right thing." Jax was right beside me, but his voice sounded like it came from the forest edge.

I stepped onto the front porch. The aroma of delicious treats was even stronger here.

The cottage looked hazy like a fine mist surrounded it—why was that? I blinked and the haze disappeared to almost nothing, but I couldn't stop staring at what remained like it was a hidden message. I should know what that was. I was sure I should.

I stiffened, suddenly realizing.

The haze was magic.

It called me inside. It wanted to trap me, or lock me up, or to do something else I couldn't begin to consider.

Barely moving my head, I looked across the lawn. The forest wasn't so far away. If I could get there, I could hide. I would not allow myself to be locked up again. Whether it was by the king or Jax, it wasn't happening. As for freeing Fergus, there was no way anyone was handing me over to the queen. And there was also no way I was leaving Fergus with her. I'd find some other way to free him if I couldn't trust Jax at his word.

I ripped myself from Jax's grasp, turning and sprinting for the cover of the trees. My legs were sore and stiff from running and from the few hours I'd spent on horseback. No matter how hard I pumped them, I couldn't move as fast as I wanted.

"Bria!" Jax's voice was both surprised and frustrated. "Come back here."

The edge of the forest drew closer.

Jax's footsteps behind grew louder.

Suddenly, everything around me exploded in green. Something smacked into my shoulder and shoved me to the ground. I hit hard. Icy snow found its way into my mouth and a burning pain shot through my left shoulder.

TWO

FAE'S BREATH. The jerk had hit me with his magic to stop me leaving. He really didn't want to let me out of his sight.

A pair of black boots crunched through the snow and stopped beside my face. "Bria? Are you okay?" Jax's voice was gentle. And apologetic.

I spat the snow from my mouth and sat up, hissing when my shoulder burned. "Fine." I cursed myself for not expecting the blast from his magic.

"I'm sorry. I can't let you leave. No hard feelings?" He held out his hand to pull me to my feet, his movements slow.

I glared at his hand and refused to take it.

"I can't fix your shoulder, but I can take some of the biting pain away. Come inside."

There was no way I was setting foot in that cottage. I pulled myself to my feet and called on my magic, glad most people—including Jax—couldn't see magic forming the same way Fergus and I could. Jax had once told me his magic was weak. A *one-shot wonder* were the words he'd used. Well, he just had his one shot, plus he used extra magic to reveal the cottage. Jax should be weak. Hopefully he hadn't undersold himself.

As Jax nodded me toward the arched cottage door, I released a ball of magic aimed at his chest. And, because one could never be too careful—my magic had never done what it should, and after months of not using it, I had no reason to think anything had changed—I grabbed his arm, pulled him toward me and kneed him in the groin.

Jax dropped to the ground like a stone, his mouth opening and closing like a fish out of water. True to form, my magic shot off in the opposite direction, away from both of us.

"No hard feelings?" I stepped over Jax just as a blast of magenta light came shooting back for us. I ducked out of the way, but it skimmed past Jax, leaving a thin trail of blood up the side of one calf as he lay on the ground with his knees pulled to his chest. My magic had hit the edge of the well, bounced off and come straight back at us.

Jax screamed in pain as my magic hit, but I was already running, even as the healer in me begged to go back and help him. "Bria! I can't heal wounds made by magic. You need to do it."

"Go ask the king," I yelled over my shoulder. "I'm sure he'll help you." He would be fine. It was nothing but a graze.

I sprinted into the forest, wishing I could find a path that was both easy to run on and easy to hide amongst. And also somewhere there were no Winter Court fae lying in wait. My legs hurt from running and my shoulder ached from the magic Jax had hit me with. What I really needed was a few hours' sleep and a decent healer. I couldn't see myself getting either.

I forced my legs to move, pushing between the pine branches and off the trail. The forest was dark. Things I could barely see moved at the edge of my vision. Jax alternated between calling my name and cursing it, his voice hoarse with pain and closer than I was comfortable with.

I ducked behind a fallen log, letting the branches of a nearby tree droop over me as I hid. With my eyes closed, I drew deep breaths and tried to keep from panting.

"Bria!" A twig snapped so close I was certain I could have reached out and touched him. I put my hand over my mouth. The last thing I needed was for him to hear me breathing.

"It's dangerous out here, Bria! Fergus will be upset if you're eaten alive by Blue Annie while I'm supposed to be looking after you!"

I didn't know what a Blue Annie was, but my imagination filled the blanks, conjuring images of fanged fae with fingernails sharper than knives stalking me in the darkness. I bit down on my tongue. Fergus might be upset if a hostile fae ate me, but he'd also be unhappy that Jax had attacked me with magic. And that I'd done the same to Jax.

Jax moved away, his voice growing quieter as he called my name and begged me to come out.

I let out my breath and sat without moving until I could no longer hear him. Then, slowly, I stood, stretched out my back and pushed between the branches.

Either my eyes had grown used to the dark, or the moon had risen. The forest no longer seemed so impossible to see, a blue hue falling around me. I placed my feet softly with each step, my eyes darting side to side as I searched for those moving creatures I saw earlier.

But there was nothing.

The forest was quiet.

And still.

Even the Azure River seemed calmer at this time of night.

I walked on, keeping to the side of the trail, walking the same direction as the water flowed—away from the cottage Jax had brought me to.

"Dearie. Would you help an old woman?"

I jumped back with a squeal, my foot millimeters from falling on the head of an old lady lying across the middle of the trail. I hadn't even seen her down there. I pressed my hand to my heart, sure the sound of it thumping was loud enough to wake the dead. "I'm sorry. I didn't see you." Her face was wrinkled and her features sharp, and long grey hair fell over her shoulders. I couldn't guess her age, but the wrinkles on her face suggested she was old enough to be someone's grandmother. Or great-grandmother.

She pushed herself to sitting and held her hand out for me to help her up. "No mind, dearie. Would you help an old woman to her feet?" As her cloak fell away, I caught a glance of the thin arm that reached out to me. It seemed only to be skin and bone, and the moonlight cast a blue hue over her body.

Mother had taught me to respect my elders. I could never walk away and leave an old woman out here on her own. I took her hand. "How did you get out here? Where are you going?"

"Home, dearie. Isn't that where we're all heading?"

I wasn't, but I neither agreed nor disagreed as her fingers clasped my hand. I pulled her to her feet, looking her over more closely. She didn't have the pointed ears of the other fae I'd seen in Faery and looked more human than fae. Which meant she was a long way from home. "What are you doing all the way out here? It's dangerous."

As she stood, her grip on my hand grew tighter until her nails—long and sharp—dug into my skin. "It's not dangerous for Annie." She cackled.

I stiffened. Jax had told me to watch out for Blue Annie. Instead, I'd run headlong into her. She didn't look dangerous. Certainly not as dangerous as anything my mind had conjured. Still, I pulled my hand back.

Her grip tightened, and she refused to release me.

Despite Jax's words, there was no way I was terrified of a little old lady I could knock over with one shove. Which is what I did. I shoved her as hard as I could, pulling back on my other hand at the same time to get away.

She didn't budge. Instead, she pulled me toward her with such force, I had to put my hand out to steady myself. It fell against her cloak. The material was soft and familiar feeling. With another cackle, she screamed, "Dinner will taste good tonight."

Dinner? There was no way I was anyone's dinner. As I balled my hand into a fist preparing to strike her, I suddenly realized what that cloak felt like.

Skin.

She was wearing a cloak made from the skin of her victims.

Nausea rolled in my gut. Then rolled again at what I was about to do.

Ignoring it, I drew my hand back and punched her face.

Her head rocked, but her grip remained strong. "You'll have to do better than that, dearie. No one escapes from Annie."

I looked around, frantic I was about to become a meal. A movement behind her caused a scream to creep up my throat. Something big was out there, just off the trail. The silhouette hovered on the other side of the trees. "Let go of me." With frantic movements, I pulled on my arm, but it did no good.

Annie dragged me along the trail like I was no heavier than a piece of paper. Even when I dropped to the ground and dug my heels in, she pulled me free, hauling me over the root covered ground on my back.

I had to get away. To do that, I needed to stop panicking and think. As I bumped along the trail, I searched for a stick, or anything else I could use as a weapon. The huge shadowy form amongst the trees caught my eye again. A shaft of moonlight fell on it, and I almost cried out.

Raven.

She was here, waiting in the shadows until I needed her.

Well, I needed her now.

I looked at Annie's hunched back as she marched along the trail. She was not an old woman, I reminded myself. And she may not have the ears, but she was most definitely fae. She intended to take me back to her home—wherever that might be—and eat me.

Spinning so I was sitting up as she dragged me along, I threw my leg out toward hers. My movement was sudden and caught her off guard. My leg snagged her ankle and she tripped, falling headlong onto the ground. She screamed as she went down, but her grip remained tight.

I jumped to my feet, told myself again she wasn't the helpless old woman she appeared to be, and kicked her in the stomach. Her grip loosened, and she wheezed out some words I didn't understand. Probably cursing my name. Still, her grip didn't relax enough for me to free myself. I kicked her again, this time aiming for her chin. Her head rocked back, and blood flowed from her mouth, black in the moonlight, but still her fingers remained locked around my wrist. She pushed up onto her knees. I aimed another kick to her stomach. And with this one, I was free.

I didn't stop to check how badly I'd injured her. I raced off the trail, branches tearing at my face and hair, and pulled myself on to Raven's waiting back.

Annie got to her feet, wobbling her way toward me faster than she had any right, and screaming curses.

I kneed Raven in the sides, and we took off at a canter through the forest.

We kept to the trail and didn't stop all night. Twice I thought Annie was behind me and pulled Raven over to hide, but she never reappeared. Neither did Jax.

Border Bridge came into view in that strange time of morning between night and dawn, when the sky is just lighter than dark. The arched stone bridge was broad with low sides and a stone pillar in the center marking the point where Seelie met Unseelie. Overnight, Raven and I had made a steady climb, and the bridge spanned a wide gorge with steep cliff faces on either side. The river, now many meters below, was deeper and faster than it had been when we first reached the lands of the Winter Court.

I might have escaped from Jax, but I didn't intend to leave Fergus without help, and this was where Jax expected an exchange of prisoners would happen. Whether or not he was telling the truth remained to be seen.

I led Raven off the trail and deeper into the woods, leaving her to graze on a small patch of wild winter grass that had pushed through the snow. With instructions to stay there and stay quiet, I found a place to hide up on the branch of a pine where I could watch both ends of the bridge as well as the trail leading up to it.

There was no movement on either side of the bridge all day. As I dozed in the weak sunlight to the lullaby of the river rushing past, I wondered if this was not the Border Bridge after all. But as the shadows grew longer, movement on the far side caught my attention.

My chest tightened. There was a man over there.

His grey uniform brought every unpleasant memory of my time locked in the Seelie prison rushing back. The fae on the other side of the bridge was one of Rhiannon's guards. But seeing that guard also made me sit up straighter. If there were guards, perhaps Fergus and Willow really were nearby, too. Maybe even Mother, though if the king was correct, she was far from here and I was happy with that, too.

A second guard wandered into view, striding out onto the bridge and stopping at the pillar in the center to look across at Unseelie. I pushed my back against the tree. There was no chance he could see me—I was looking at him between thick clumps of pine needles—but I didn't want to test fate, either.

My mind raced. Until I saw the guards, I hadn't really believed the queen might bring Fergus and Willow here today. But those guards meant that was likely, and that Fergus and Willow were also here, or almost here. I just needed to come up with a way to rescue them.

Horse hooves along the trail behind me made me turn, and Jax rode by with someone walking on the far side of him. I sucked in a breath, surprised he was here. Without me to use as a swap, I'd talked myself into believing he had no reason to come.

Perhaps I was wrong about his motives. Or his plan.

He stopped at the foot of the bridge and dismounted. In a voice too soft to hear, he spoke to the person beside him, but I couldn't see the person's reaction because Flame shielded him from view. Jax glared at Rhiannon's guard, hands clenching and unclenching at his sides. Rhiannon's guard stared back a moment before turning and strolling away.

The moment the guard reached the far side, and seeming to appear from nowhere, Queen Rhiannon stepped onto the bridge. Each of her hands were clamped around the wrist of a prisoner on either side of her. A sack covered both prisoner's heads, and they shuffled forward slowly, heads bowed.

My breath came fast. I'd had one of those thrown over my head the night the queen tried to take me, too. I'd kicked and screamed and tried to get free. It hadn't worked, and the queen's guards had thrown me over the back of a horse, only for the king's soldiers to steal me back.

The two with the queen today walked beside her as if they had no other place they'd rather be. Or as if they had no energy to defy her.

Jax's shoulders went rigid, his body as still as a stone, though I imagined his eyes followed the progress of the three on the bridge.

The queen moved, drawing my eyes back to her and her prisoners. She wore a deep red dress with jewels sparkling on the bodice in the late afternoon sunlight. By contrast, her prisoner's clothing was ripped and dirty. I was certain it was Fergus and Willow, though it was impossible to tell for sure. All I could see was that one prisoner was taller than the queen, the other shorter.

The queen's voice floated across the river, louder than it should have been and carried by red magic which disappeared with her voice. "Do you have your prisoner?"

"I do." Pale green magic carried Jax's voice back to her.

The queen gave a single nod. "Then have her walk across to Seelie."

Jax's hands were balled so tight, his knuckles were white. He lifted his chin. "Once you release your prisoners to walk over to Unseelie."

A faint smile pulled at her lips. "As you wish." Faded red magic pooled around her, but she and her prisoners remained unmoving.

Despite demanding the queen release her prisoners at the same time as him, Jax pushed his companion forward without waiting for the queen to do the same. I stood up on the branch, searching for a better view. Now he had no one to bargain with should Rhiannon not keep her word. It made no sense.

And who was his prisoner? Who did Rhiannon want so much she'd exchange them for the Unseelie Prince and Princess? The person was dressed all in black, from their pants to their cloak. And the hood of that cloak covered their head.

As Jax's prisoner reached the middle of the bridge, Jax let out a breath and his shoulders relaxed. My brain whirred. Another piece I didn't understand in this strange puzzle.

Suddenly, a bolt of bright orange magic flew from a guard behind the queen. It burrowed into the shoulder of Jax's prisoner. The prisoner cried out—a distinctly female sound—and dropped to her knees. Another two fast shots followed, and Jax's prisoner fell face first onto the bridge where I could no longer see her.

"Bria!" I didn't need magic to hear or recognize that voice from the other side of the bridge. It was Fergus. The way his voice broke as he yelled made the hair on my neck stand up—he must be able to see through the fabric of the sack.

I suddenly understood Jax's plan. When he no longer had me to swap, he'd found someone else who would pretend to be me. And Fergus had a front row view, watching the very thing Jax told me wouldn't happen. Fergus believed the queen's guards had just injured me. He pulled against the queen's grip, dropping to his knees as he called my name again. The Queen's lips were pursed as she watched the girl in the center of the bridge.

Another blast of magic shot along the bridge. I couldn't see where it hit, but from the cry Fergus made, I imagined Jax's prisoner—my proxy—was now dead, or very close to it. There was no way she could survive so many lethal blasts of magic. Especially when with each shot, huge chunks of the stone bridge dropped with a splash into the water below.

Jax made a noise and reached out for something in front of him, his arms wide as if he were about to hug someone. But there was no one there. No one was even close to him.

Had the queen produced a glamour he couldn't see through?

The answer should have been no. He'd told me he was immune to that sort of magic. Yet, his actions over the past few minutes indicated otherwise.

As Jax's hand swept through thin air, he seemed to realize she had tricked him. He pressed the heels of each hand into his eye sockets, his shoulders rising and falling as he pulled in some deep breaths. He drew his hands away and yelled at the queen. "We had a deal!" He didn't need magic to carry his voice this time, it was loud enough without.

Rhiannon shrugged. "I changed my mind. But here, take this one. And don't say I never do the right thing." She pushed the shorter prisoner—Willow, I guessed—out onto the bridge. The prisoner took two steps out of the queen's grasp, then stopped and pulled the sack off her head.

Willow stood still, blinking against the bright light as two fae guards pushed past her, jogging single file onto the bridge ahead of her.

"Willow," I breathed, my heart somersaulting. We were definitely getting one of them back today. Both if I had my way.

Every part of Willow's face was bruised, and her blonde hair was matted around her face. She let the sack fall from her fingers, and it caught on the breeze and floated down to the river far below. Taking a breath so deep her shoulders lifted, she spread her arms at right angles to her body and started across the bridge with small steps.

Like she was on a balancing beam.

Like the bridge was so damaged by the blasts of magic the queen's guards had used, there was very little left to stand upon.

The guards—walking one behind the other, even though without the damage there should have been room to walk side-by-side—drew closer to the center marker. I wasn't sure what they were doing. Coming to attack Jax? He clearly didn't think so, stepping onto the bridge and yelling, "Come on, Willow. Faster." With each step Willow took, Jax moved closer to her. He'd crept so far onto the bridge, he was almost at the border marker. The guards rushed toward him, but he seemed not to care. He was totally focused on Willow, one hand reaching out for her as he encouraged her forward.

The guards reached the border marker. One bent, ducking out of sight behind the stone sides of the bridge.

Jax's entire body tensed and I suddenly understood why he was so desperate that Willow hurry. He was about to be discovered.

The guard got to his feet, turning to yell back at the queen. "It's not her!"

The queen's smile came slowly to her face. "Of course, it's not." Her gaze shifted to Jax. "You must think me very stupid to believe that I could mistake someone so much taller for my niece." Rhiannon's hand moved so fast I barely saw it. Red magic flared, and the bridge exploded around Jax. Stones flew in every direction and Jax dropped through the bottom into the churning water below. She'd known it wasn't me, but had killed Jax's prisoner anyway. Now she was taking her anger out on Jax.

Willow screamed, then whirled to face the queen. "How dare you!"

A faint smile pulled at the queen's lips and she shrugged. With a wave of her hand, another blast of red magic hit the bridge.

And Willow followed Jax into the water.

THREE

I MOVED on the branch, watching helplessly from my place beside the bridge as Willow hit the raging water and the swirling current dragged her under.

Then I dropped onto the ground and ran.

I sprinted across the trail, jumped over logs, ducked under branches. And hoped I recalled exactly where I'd left Raven. She was my only chance of getting down to the water to search for Willow.

Like she knew I wanted her, Raven pushed through the thick foliage and waited as I pulled myself onto her back.

"We have to find Willow, Raven. Can you help me?" I talked to her because I needed to talk to someone to keep myself sane. The river was mean and angry. If Willow even survived the fall, I couldn't imagine her lasting long in that current.

We raced along the trail, searching for a place we could get down to the river. I got occasional glimpses of the water, I even thought I might have seen Willow once, but there was never any way to get down the steep cliff face to reach her.

Raven ran so fast I was certain I was going to fall from her back. I gave up on the reins and weaved my fingers into her mane, clinging tight until she finally slowed, stopping at a place where, long ago, erosion had pulled a chunk of the cliff down to the river. It had taken with it trees that grew at the very edge of the forest, and many of them—plus some newer, smaller ones—still grew on the mound of dirt that had slipped down the hill. Better still, a trail—steep and rough—led down to the water.

I leaped from her back and ran, stumbling down the path. I used branches and tree trunks to slow my descent just enough that I wasn't out of control, and when the trail flattened, I could have kissed Raven for bringing me here.

High cliffs towered over the place she'd brought me to, but the river was narrow and fast-flowing. The large boulders at the edge were flattened by

years of erosion. Easy to walk across, and hopefully, a good place for a rescue.

I searched the rocks until I found a long, thick
branch and dragged it across the boulders to the
edge of the river. Upstream, I caught sight of
Willow. Her blonde hair was visible for a few
seconds before she dropped beneath the raging
current and out of sight.

The next time she surfaced, I yelled her name
and waved my arms. She raised an arm. I didn't
know if that meant she'd seen me, or if she was
just trying to keep her head above the water. As
she ducked under again, I heaved one end of the
branch out where I hoped she'd resurface. The moment she came up, I shoved it as close to her as I
could manage.

She gripped onto it. Her weight and the force
of the water almost pulled me in. I dug my heels
into the rocks, bent my knees, and silently asked
the stars for help.

The rapids flowed over Willow's head and all I
could see were her hands on the stick. Water spray
hit my face, icy cold, and the stick slipped along
my palms, ripping my skin. I gripped it tighter,
ignoring the pain. "Hold on!" With gritted teeth,
I pulled as hard as I could, yelling but unsure if
she could hear me above the raging water. "Kick
your legs." I moved backward across the rocks, the

water slowly giving her up, until suddenly, I was pulling her up on the rock beside me.

She collapsed into a heap, her breathing heavy.

"Are you all right?" I ran my fingers over her body, searching for broken bones, but there were none. Thank the stars.

She coughed. "I'm fine. Jax?" Her voice was rough.

I shook my head. "I haven't seen him." And hadn't wasted a thought on him since Willow went into the water.

She pointed upstream. "Rock."

"Jax is on a rock?"

She nodded and gripped my hand. "Help him. Please."

I shook my head. What I could see of upstream before the river turned out of sight were canyon walls that came right down to the water. There was no way I could pick my way along the edge to find Jax because there was no edge. Even less chance if I was holding my rescue stick, which was the only way I could guide him from the water. "I can't. There's no way—"

"Raven." Willow's eyes were closed and her chest heaved with the effort to catch her breath.

I raised my eyebrows. "You know Raven's here?"

She gave a faint smile. "Saw you riding her like Blue Annie was on your tail. Fly her to Jax."

I took her hand. I had to tell her what he'd done last night. "Willow, Jax is—"

"Please, Bria. He'll die if you don't help him. There's no way out of the river until it meets the sea. And by then he'll be dead." She rolled on her side and rested her cheek on the boulder beneath her. "No one deserves to die like that."

I scrubbed a hand down my face. It was Fergus' magic that gave Raven the ability to fly. His magic had probably been suppressed for the past three months, leaving very little for the horses of the Wild Hunt. I'd planned to use Raven to search for Fergus the moment Willow was safe and before the Queen had time to drag Fergus back to her castle. Wasting even a drop of time or magic searching for Jax was less that I had for Fergus.

Willow squeezed my hand. "I'd be forever grateful. So would Fergus."

It wasn't the gratitude of Fergus or Willow that drove me to do as she asked. It was knowing how close the three of them were. They'd been there for each other all their lives, and I almost understood why Jax would hand me over to save them.

I left Willow—pale and panting—on the rocks, promising to return soon, and climbed the steep trail up to where Raven stood waiting like she knew exactly what I wanted from her. I climbed on her back. "Let's go get Jax."

I rode back up the trail we'd raced down moments before, looking for a gap in the foliage. The horses of the Wild Hunt as a group got their ability to fly from the leader's magic, but that just gave them the ability. Making them fly was their rider's job, though I'd never done it on my own before. Fergus had always been with me when the horses flew. This time, I would have to make it happen.

Before I commanded Raven to step off the side of the cliff, I called on my magic, imagining it forming beneath her feet to give her something to run on. With a racing heart and white knuckles, I asked her to fly.

She leapt into the air and my stomach dropped as we dipped swiftly down toward the water. My eyes snapped shut and I wrapped my fingers tighter into Raven's mane, bracing for the impact that never came. The wind rushed past, catching us and lifting us up.

We were flying!

My eyes fluttered open, but my vision was all wrong. Without turning my head, I could see everything around me; the river, the Seelie forest in front of me, even some of the Winter Court lands behind me. The blue of the river was so much deeper, the green of the Seelie forest lush and bright. But I had no choice in what I looked at.

Because I was seeing the world through Raven's eyes.

It was beautiful.

My heart beat in time with hers, fast and joyous, and adrenaline—Raven's adrenaline—pumped through my veins. She loved flying this way as much as I did, probably more. The connection between us was like nothing I'd ever felt before, and it was infectious. I wanted to keep this connection forever. It made flying with her even better.

I blinked and my vision was my own again. My magic that helped get her into the air wasn't flowing beneath her feet, the way I'd expected it might. A ribbon of magenta flowed from my heart to hers. I was a part of her, and she a part of me.

Raven ran just above the river, water spraying my hands and face. Still, I couldn't help but smile. I loved riding Raven this way, even if I was going to collect someone who hated me enough to hand me over to the queen who wanted me dead.

The rock Jax had hauled himself onto was in the center of the river. The water parted around it, currents eddying either side, white and angry. He stood when he saw me and raised his hand, dropping it back to his side when he realized it was me rather than another of his Wild Hunt friends. Probably thought I'd leave him there. Probably knew I'd considered it.

There was no place for Raven to land, but she slowed, and I held out my hand. Jax eyed it warily, then gripped hold and pulled himself onto Raven's back behind me. Raven turned and followed the river downstream to the place I'd rescued Willow.

We didn't speak and Jax slid off Raven's back before we'd even stopped moving, dropping down to crouch next to Willow. She was sitting up, her arms wrapped around her body as she shivered against the cold. She looked pale and small, her lips blue. Not a thing like the glamorous girl I'd met at two of the biggest events in Unseelie.

Jax crouched behind her and lifted the back of her wet shirt. Piercing the skin of one shoulder was a small suppressor. The iron rod that Rhiannon's guards had inserted into her body weakened her magic so only a minute piece of her massive power remained, and she was no longer a threat to her captors.

I gasped. How had I not thought to check for that before I left her? It was much smaller than the ones I'd removed from Fergus and the way her wet shirt was rucked up over her back, it had been hidden. But still I should have thought to look for it. "Sorry, Willow. I should have removed that before..."

She shook her head. "I preferred you went after Jax. It's fine."

"It's not fine," spat Jax, glaring at me. "Why would you leave her like this?"

I glared at him from my seat upon Raven. "Oh, I don't know. Maybe I was too terrified to think straight after someone I thought was a friend tried to hurt me last night before taking me to the queen to die." But that wasn't the reason. Jax was right. It was lazy for a healer not to check a patient properly, and I was too embarrassed to admit it.

Willow looked between us, her brow furrowing. "What's going on?"

I shook my head. "Doesn't matter. I'm going to get Fergus back. I'll see you later." I turned Raven upstream.

"Bria? What?" Willow struggled to her feet. "You can't go into Seelie.

I shook my head. "I can and I will. You sit down and let..." I almost choked on Jax's name I was so annoyed with him. "Let Jax remove that suppressor."

She looked between me and Jax, like she thought he might go with me to help. I already

knew he wouldn't. If he'd had another plan to rescue Fergus, he would have put it into action last
night when he lost me.

My voice was gentle when I spoke again. "It's
okay, Willow. I'll bring him back. I promise." I
clicked my tongue and Raven moved off before
I had to see the look on Willow's face. That was
a big promise. Possibly a hollow one. But I had a
plan.

And I had two things on my side.

It was less than five minutes since Jax and
Willow fell from the bridge—the queen's guards
couldn't have taken Fergus far in that time—and
I had a horse that could fly.

Of course, I didn't know how long that horse
would be able to fly, so this was going to have to
be fast.

We followed the river, sweeping beneath the remains of the Border Bridge—which was empty of
people. The moment I decided it was time to rise
high above the water, higher than the tallest trees
in the Winter Court, Raven did it. I didn't need to
use words or gestures, our connection directed her
as if she were a part of me. I scanned the Seelie forest, searching below for the queen's party.

They weren't hard to find. The forest on the
Seelie side of the border was thin, fading to rolling
green meadows not far from the river.

A group of Seelie soldiers rode on a trail away from the bridge. And Fergus stumbled along in the center of them, surrounded. The queen was gone. Probably already back at her castle by whatever magic she used to move herself around. I silently thanked the stars I didn't have her to deal with as well.

I didn't have unlimited time for Raven to stay in the air, and if I waited too much longer, the sun would be gone, and I'd lose my advantage. It was now or never.

I called on my magic, waiting while it pooled around me before leaning forward and wrapping one arm around Raven's neck. "Let's go get Fergus."

As Raven swooped down toward the party of guards, I released my magic. It shot out of my hand, the blast burrowing into the pristine hill far to the left of the guards, never a threat of hurting any of them.

Every person in the party jumped. Then they turned in small circles, searching for the attacker as they called on their magic, a different color forming around each guard. The horses flared their nostrils and stomped their feet, uncomfortable with the threat they hadn't yet seen.

Only Fergus knew where to look. He lifted his eyes for a moment, squinting into the sun and probably unable to see me, before dropping his gaze to the ground. It didn't matter. He wouldn't give me away—I had the sun at my back. Even if the guards expected an attack from above—which they didn't—they couldn't see me.

I let off another blast, this one shooting over their heads and hitting the ground on the other side of the group. I couldn't control where it landed, and at the moment, it didn't much matter. All I wanted was a diversion.

One guard let his own magic fly. It shot along the ground and away from me. I smiled. He had no idea where I was.

Raven and I swooped down toward Fergus. Still no one looked up, making us the perfect surprise attack.

As she ran above them, her hooves hit a soldier in the head. He fell beneath us, without so much as a shout.

Now they saw us.

I leaned over and took Fergus' outstretched hand, dragging him away from the guards. One of them caught hold of his foot, but Fergus kicked him off and I hauled him onto Raven's back.

A ball of magic came our way. *Fly left,* I commanded Raven inside my head. Raven ducked to the left and the magic shot straight past. Galloping hard, I silently directed Raven toward the sun, and she rose over Seelie. Another ball of magic came at us, but I urged Raven on until we were out of range.

I let out a whoop. "We did it!"

Behind me, Fergus wrapped his arms around my waist and rested his forehead on my shoulder. My heart was thumping from the adrenaline of the rescue, but his touch made it lurch in my chest. Many times over the past months, I'd wondered if I'd see him again, and now he was right here with me, his arms around my waist. A stupid smile crept onto my face. I turned my head, looking at his messy black hair blowing in the wind, a sight I could easily watch all day long. He must have felt my movement, because he looked up and smiled, and my stomach fluttered.

One of his eyes was black and his lip was swollen and bloody. But worse than the injuries I could see were the ones I could only guess at. His smile was tired and every movement an effort, even if he was attempting to hide that from me. There were suppressors in his back, draining his magic and his energy. I put one hand over his. I couldn't put into words how good it was to have him beside me again, but he needed medical attention. And he needed it now.

We flew downstream along the river until I found Willow and Jax, exactly where I left them.

Willow lay on her stomach on the boulder. Jax was on his back beside her. I waved and hoped they'd make their way up to the trail beside the river. I couldn't stop on the rocks in case Raven's magic ran out—Fergus was in no condition to climb the steep hill back up to the trail, and there was no way any of us could drag him up.

We landed on the trail at the very top of the cliff among the pine trees. Fergus slid down and waited on wobbling legs for me to do the same. His face was almost as pale as the snow on the ground, and he was skinnier than he'd been three months ago. "I can't believe you just did that." He shook his head, then wrapped his arms around me, resting his chin on my head.

"Did what?" I sank into him, inhaling his scent. For three months I'd thought about this reunion and had wondered if it would ever happen.

"Plucked me out of the middle of a group of Rhiannon's best guards." He pulled back, a grin growing on his lips. I wasn't certain, but in the moments since we'd landed there seemed to be more color in his cheeks.

I shrugged. "I guess I had the advantage with the horse and the sunlight."

"And the outstanding use of magic."

I narrowed my eyes. "You must be delirious if you think my magic was good."

"I'm not delirious." He threw an arm over my shoulder and I drew in a sharp breath. Mostly, I'd been ignoring the burning pain where Jax's magic hit me last night, but that was impossible when Fergus touched it.

He pulled back. "Are you hurt? I can heal it."

"I'm fine." He wasn't healing anything. Or using his magic until I was certain it wouldn't drain him completely. I didn't want him to end up almost dead again.

Fergus smiled, then his knees buckled.

I caught him around his waist and helped him to the ground. "Suppressors?"

He nodded.

I moved behind him and pulled up his shirt. "She really didn't want you escaping, did she?" Last time, the queen had used two suppressors to keep Fergus' magic in check. This time, there were four—two on each shoulder blade.

Fergus blew out a laugh. "Guess not."

Each bar had been in his body for so long that the skin on his shoulder blades was raw, red, and angry, the sores weeping. I'd seen some bad wounds as a healer, but this was right up there. Taking them out was going to hurt both of us.

I steeled myself, and without warning him, took hold of the barbed ends of one bar and pulled. The burning pain I remembered returned, but it wasn't as bad as last time, and I had the cap off and the bar out within seconds.

Fergus let out a sigh, his body relaxing a fraction. "Only three to go."

The following three came out almost as easily, ripping and burning my hands with each touch. The damage they did to me was nothing compared to the state of Fergus' back.

He collapsed forward in the dirt the moment they were out. "Thank you."

I touched his shoulder. "Rest. I'll see what's taking Willow and Jax so long." I was certain they'd seen me. They should have climbed the trail by now.

I made my way down, expecting to meet them coming up, but it was just me, the birdsong and the roaring river. Down on the boulders, they were still lying as they had when I flew overhead.

I raced to them, thinking for a second they were both dead. Then I saw Willow's chest rise and fall. "Willow? What's going on?" I lifted my voice above the noise of the river.

She turned her head. "Bria. You came back?"

"Of course I did. And I brought Fergus." I crouched beside her. Her shirt was rucked up over her shoulders, the suppresser still imbedded in her skin. "Why didn't Jax remove this?" I glanced his way. He hadn't moved since I arrived, not even to crack his eyes open.

"He tried, but he was too weak. There is a wound on his leg. From magic."

I pressed my lips together. My magic. Clearly, Jax hadn't told Willow that yet.

"I tried to heal him, but..." She shook her head. As a princess and therefore one of the strongest in the kingdom, she could heal wounds made by magic. Just not while she was weakened from wearing a suppressor.

"It's okay. I'll get it out for you." I stared at the iron in her back. Nausea rose inside me at the thought of touching another of these, but we needed to get back to Fergus, and that wouldn't happen unless I helped Willow. Neither of them were currently well enough to get themselves up that hill without help.

I steeled myself again. My hands—bloody and burned from removing Fergus' suppressors—hovered over the one in Willow's back for a moment and she stiffened. She knew this was going to hurt. "I'll try to be gentle."

"Do what you have to." She spoke like her teeth were already gritted.

I took hold of the barbed ends, burning pain biting into my hands and running right up my arms, but the suppressor was apart a moment later. I pulled it from Willow's skin and tossed it into the river.

She let out a huge breath and pushed herself up to sit. "Thank you."

I held out my hand to help her to her feet. "We need to get out of here." What she needed was rest, but I wasn't sure we had that luxury. At least, not until we were safely out of the forest and back on Fergus' island.

She refused my hand and looked at Jax. His eyes were open and his chest moved with each breath, but other than that, he was still. "Bria, can you roll up his pant leg?" She was still weak, her movements slow. To get up that hill, I needed them both on their feet and moving as soon as possible.

I crouched beside Jax and did as she asked. The place where my magic had skimmed his leg was burnt and bloody, but the surrounding skin looked like something had eaten it. I drew in a breath. "Why is he reacting like this?"

Willow frowned. "What do you mean?"

I shrugged. His magic had hit me last night, and though I couldn't see the wound on my shoulder, I knew it looked nothing like his. If it did, I wouldn't be able to move. "It wasn't that bad last night. Just a scratch."

"This is how a wound made by another fae's magic looks. Some wounds take longer to get to this point, some take less, but they all get here, eventually." She moved her hand above Jax's leg and yellow magic flared. At the top end of the wound, the flesh knit together, the redness disappearing.

"Willow, stop!" I put my hand up in front of her. Fergus had used his magic instead of resting when the suppressors came off last time and almost died.

Her hand above Jax's leg didn't move, but she met my eyes. "He'll die if I don't finish healing him." There was a long way to go. Only the very top end of the wound was better.

"You'll die if you do."

She shook her head, her lips set in a hard line. "Ferg's here. If this goes wrong, he'll save me. But hopefully he won't need to."

"But—"

My protest was cut off as the rock beside Jax's foot exploded in a ball of dark green light, a piece the size of a shoe rocketing between Willow and me.

I jumped and grabbed hold of Willow's arm, adrenaline punching through me. "What in the stars...?"

She climbed to her feet, wobbling as she pulled at Jax's hand to get him to sit. "Someone's trying to kill us." Her eyes flitted across the river to the top of the cliff.

I followed her gaze to find a group of the queen's guards standing up there. As I watched, a blast of orange shot from one of their hands. "Run!"

I grabbed Jax, pulling him to his feet. To his credit, once he was upright, he moved under his own steam. Thank goodness, because Willow and I had no chance of carrying him up that hill. Willow jogged beside him, and I followed.

Orange magic splashed into the water just behind me, sending spray up and over us.

"They're too far away to aim properly," Willow yelled over her shoulder. "Once we get to the forest and they can't see us, we'll be safe."

Another blast hit the rock beside Willow's foot. She screamed and stumbled. I grabbed her arm on the way past, pulling her with me. A ball of aqua magic quickly followed by one of fiery orange and another of pale blue exploded around me. It was only a matter of time until they hit one of us.

Willow's knees buckled, and she slipped from my grasp and onto the ground. I bent and put a hand around her waist, trying to pull her up. "I can't. Go without me."

I shook my head. I hadn't gone to all the effort to get her brother home just to leave her here as target practice for those Seelie jerks. "Stand up. We're almost there." We were almost at the bottom of the hill, at least. And, like she'd said, the trees around the trail on the way up would offer some protection.

Gritting my teeth and using my body weight as leverage, I hauled her to her feet. No one was staying here. Not if I could help it.

There was a loud crack as magic sheared through a tree on the hill. It fell, crashing down onto the rocks beside us with so much force the impact made the ground shake.

I swallowed down a scream and ran with my arm around Willow and just a few steps behind Jax over the rocks and onto the trail.

Blast after blast of magic hit around us, shaving branches from trees or burrowing into the dirt. Willow grew heavier with each step until she was barely holding her own weight and I was dragging her up the trail. Her head lolled forward, jolting with each step. She hadn't listened. She'd used too much magic trying to heal Jax.

I didn't know how I was going to make it up the hill. It was so steep that walking myself up stole my breath. Carrying Willow made it almost impossible.

A movement at the top of the trail drew my eye. Fergus stood up there, bracing himself with one hand against a tree and looking like he wanted to kill something—but only if he could stay upright long enough to do so. That was enough to give me another burst of energy. I didn't want him coming down here. I especially didn't want him using his magic. The only option to stop him was getting all of us back up to him.

I dragged Willow up the last of the trail and found a concealed place to sit her down to rest. Jax hugged Fergus, then stepped away, his eyes on Willow.

"What happened?" asked Fergus, his eyes scanning over his sister, then me before taking a final glance at Jax.

"Seelie Guards. From across the river." I leaned over Willow, checking her breathing. It was there, but faint. I pulled a hand down my face. She'd used too much magic. The same as her brother had done last time he was released from a suppressor.

As a princess of the Seelie court, I should be able to make her better. But my magic didn't work like everyone else's, and there was no chance I was trying it. I'd just as likely kill her as heal her. I could however heal her in a different way. "I'm going to need some nightbalm berries. Do they grow near here?" I looked between Fergus and Jax.

Fergus' legs wobbled and he sat down so fast, I wasn't sure if he'd fallen. I watched him until he held up a hand. "I'm fine." He blinked twice. "No nightbalm here." He nodded over my shoulder. "They never grow this close to a river."

"How far would I need to go to find some?" Willow looked so pale. She needed help, and fast.

Fergus shrugged. He was blinking hard and looked almost as spaced out as his sister.

I turned to Jax, who was still watching Willow. If he'd give me directions, I could take Raven and find some. "Jax?"

He looked up, like he hadn't heard the previous conversation.

"Nightbalm?" I prompted.

"None here. You need to go back toward the border with Iadrun. Or into Seelie. Either way, it'll take you hours."

The forest lit up with the bright flash of Seelie magic. A branch high above cracked. I grabbed Willow and pulled her farther off the trail. Jax and Fergus jumped to their feet, following. "Get behind a tree," I yelled, my eyes falling on Raven, an idea forming. "Jax, is your horse still at the bridge?"

He blinked as he looked up, then shook his head. "Flame...? I guess so."

"And you have enough magic to fly her back to Lanwick Island?" I needed to ask Fergus the same thing.

"Probably ... maybe." Jax shook his head. "No." His face had paled since we reached the top of the hill, and his hands shook when he unclasped them from his lap.

I went to where he sat and pulled up his pant leg. Willow had only had time to heal the very top of the wound, the rest was as red and angry as before.

"Willow was interrupted," he mumbled.

I cursed, looking around the forest. I had three injured fae, and one—possibly two if I could get it back here—magical horses to transport them on. How far Jax's horse could take us was up for debate. "Do you have enough magic to get Flame to the Unseelie castle?"

Jax nodded.

Okay, that was an option. "What would the king do to me if I took you all back to the castle?"

"You don't want to know," mumbled Jax, his eyelids drooping.

Fergus shook his head. "He's right. You don't."

"Well, we have to go somewhere." I looked at Fergus. "Willow and Jax need you to heal them and you can't rest and regain your magic here with Seelie guards shooting at us." I thought about Blue Annie. "Not to mention the other things that come out in this forest at night. Any ideas where we could go?"

Both Jax and Fergus rested against different trees, heads back and eyes shut. Neither answered.

I pushed away the panic that tried to bubble up into my throat. Everything was fine. "Jax. Can you call Flame to us?"

His eyes were closed and he didn't answer. No one answered. That was fine, too. I could do this. I licked my lips and whistled, the same way I'd seen Fergus and Jax call their horses. Raven came to me immediately, and when, after a few minutes waiting, Flame didn't appear, I tried again.

"She won't come to you." Willow's eyes were closed and her voice so weak I thought I'd imagined it.

I replied anyway, mostly to keep the panic at bay. "Why not? Fergus and Jax do this all the time. And it worked for Raven."

Willow didn't need to answer. The reason was as clear as if she'd written it on the ground in front of me. Flame wasn't my horse. I had no connection with her. Fergus had a connection with all the Wild Hunt's horses. He could call any of them. The only other person who could call Flame was Jax.

Wary of making Fergus use his magic, I crouched beside Jax and shook his shoulder. His eyes cracked open. "Can you call Flame please? If I don't have to go back to the bridge and get her, we can get out of here sooner."

His eyelids dropped and he gave no answer.

"I could help Willow sooner."

He opened his eyes and sat up straighter. Without a word to me, he gave a loud whistle. A few minutes later, and followed by a volley of colored magic from across the river, Flame appeared.

I let out my breath. That was one problem solved.

The next might be a little more difficult.

I crouched in front of Fergus and touched his shoulder. His eyes shot open. "Can you help me get Willow onto Raven's back?" Between him and Jax, he looked the more likely to lift her.

He nodded and, with my help, stood. Between us we maneuvered her up, laying her forward so her head rested on the back of Raven's neck. Fergus produced a rope, the faint glow of his light blue magic appearing with it. I cast him a disapproving look. I didn't want him using his magic and ending up in the same condition as Willow.

He ignored my glare and tied Willow onto Raven. "Safer this way."

It was. Which was why I hadn't argued.

I crouched in front of Jax. "Jax. Get up." I gave his shoulder a shove—less gentle than I would have been before last night—and his eyelids fluttered open. "Flame's here. You need to get on her." Another blast of magic hit somewhere to our left. Those Seelie guards needed to give up and go home to their families. They'd be lucky to hit us when we were so far from the river and the only way for them to reach us was if they circled back and crossed the damaged Border Bridge, which they wouldn't do because they weren't allowed to cross into Unseelie lands. All they were currently doing was wasting their magic.

Jax nodded.

I held out my hand and pulled him to his feet.

He and Fergus climbed onto Flame though neither looked well enough to stay there long.

"Where are we going?" asked Fergus.

I walked over to Raven. "Just follow me." I was taking them to the Unseelie castle. I'd drop them off, yell for help, then run to Iadrun where I'd find a village to hide from the king, and hope I made it—he'd only kept me alive all these months as bargaining power with the queen, and he no longer required that.

This was the only option that would save all three lives—the king was the only other person in Unseelie who had enough magic to heal Willow and Jax, and to make sure Fergus didn't kill himself by trying to help them.

I climbed on Raven and called on my magic, making an immediate connection with her. Jax did the same with Flame, but where my ribbon of magic was easily a hand-width thick, the connection between Jax and Flame was as thin as a thread. I didn't know if that was normal between the two of them—I'd never seen the magic between rider and horse until I saw it between me and Raven. Now it seemed I could see that same connection in others.

We exited through the canopy of the forest, the night sky encasing us. Flame flew just behind. I wasn't sure if it was my imagination, or if she looked to be struggling. The dark outline of the forest stretched for miles below, snow thicker on the trees as we moved away from Seelie flying above the Winter Court lands.

When Flame dipped suddenly, dropping like a stone toward the forest, I didn't stop to think. I threw another ribbon of my magic out toward her, connecting with her before Fergus had the chance to do it.

The connection with Flame differed from my connection with Raven, more distant, like she wanted me to know she preferred Jax. I sent calm thoughts to her and showed her I was helping Jax, hoping to ease her worries. Slowly, she accepted my magic and allowed me to work with her.

I didn't relax until the Unseelie castle came into view, the imposing form sending light spilling in every direction.

Willow turned her head, her lips moving as she spoke.

I leaned closer, but couldn't hear her above the rushing wind, so I smiled like I understood, hoping it would be enough for her to close her eyes and rest.

Raven made a sudden sharp turn to the left, tracking away from the castle. "Where are you going, girl? We need to get Fergus and Willow to the castle."

She snorted in response.

Willow smiled softly and closed her eyes.

FOUR

"WHAT IS this place? I feel like I know it."
Fergus slid from Flame's back, his knees giving
out the moment he touched the ground. He sat
down heavily amongst the ivy growing around
his feet.

I pressed my lips together, biting back the
reprimand I wanted to give. He looked worse than
he had before we climbed on the horses, even
though he'd promised using them wouldn't tax his
magic.

I shook my head. "I don't know. I let Raven
bring us here." *Here* was deep in the forest, in the
overgrown garden of a cottage so old and unloved
the front door was hanging off its hinges. An icy

wind blew across the yard, not quite as cold as the Winter Court had been, but almost.

Jax dropped from his horse to sit on the dirt beside Fergus. "You know we're in Iadrun?" Disgust dripped from his voice. I wasn't sure if it was for me or because we were in human lands. And right now, I didn't have time to care, not with how sickly all three of them looked.

It had surprised me when Raven flew toward the Faery border that sparkled in the moonlight. Even more so when she rode up to a narrow part that didn't sparkle at all and pushed through. We weren't far from Holbeck—maybe an hour's walk to my home—but I'd never seen this cottage in my life, and I'd spent a lot of time as a child exploring, hunting and playing in this part of the forest. "We should be safe here." Safe from the fae that roamed Faery at night, anyway.

Fergus made a noise in his throat that I could only decipher as disagreement. He'd pulled his knees up to his chest and sat with his head bowed forward. He was right. I had no idea if we were any safer here than had we stayed in Faery. The sensible thing would have been to take them all to the Unseelie castle for the king to look after them as planned. But the way things stood, Fergus' magic was so depleted we couldn't get the horses in the air until after he'd rested, which meant we were stuck here for at least a few hours.

I helped Willow off Raven, sat her beside the boys, then approached the cottage. I couldn't make my feet move faster than a crawl while every scenario of who or what might wait inside ran through my mind; Blue Annie, the king, Rhiannon, some other dangerous fae beast I had yet to meet.

I stepped onto the rotted front porch. If I didn't watch where I placed my feet, I would fall right through the floorboards, and we didn't need another injury. I knocked on the half-open door. "Hello? Anyone here?"

When there was no answer, I pushed the door open and stepped inside.

Even by only the light of the moon, the cottage was as neglected inside as it seemed from the outside. The entrance hall—which for some reason, I expected to hold a staircase, even though the house was clearly single level—led off on one side to a bedroom with an old bedframe complete with stained mattress in one corner, and to a living area on the other. There were two more rooms farther down the hall, which I imagined were bedrooms or a kitchen. Layers of dirt and dust covered the floor, and the hearth looked as if it had been many years since it had seen a fire. Still, inside we'd be out of the icy wind, and away from prying eyes. In here, I could attempt to heal my friends.

I went back out and helped each of them across the rotten porch and inside. The only items in the living room were an empty coal bucket for the fire and an old chaise lounge that was losing its stuffing at one end. I lay Willow on the chair—both the boys were too tall to fit. I took Fergus into the bedroom and helped him onto the bed, my worry for him spiking when he mumbled, "Make sure you get enough nightbalm berries for one extra."

I smiled blandly, my heart almost beating out of my chest. If he was asking for them, he knew he was in a bad way. "Let's hope we don't need them."

There was no furniture left for Jax to lie on. I helped him inside and sat him against the wall just inside the living room door where he could see Willow. Guilt punched me in the stomach. It was my fault he was so unwell. I hadn't meant to hurt him, but it was still my magic that was doing the damage.

With a final glance at them all, I raced out the door and into the dark forest. Unlike the last time I'd searched for herbs, I was now as good as in my back yard and it took only minutes to find a stand of nightbalm berries among the oaks, elms and pine trees. I held out the end of my shirt and dropped the berries inside. Then, almost as quickly, I located some dalliagrass for pain. I didn't know how to fix the wound I'd given Jax, but at least I could help with any pain he might be in until Willow or Fergus were well enough to help him.

I started my mad dash back to the cottage, only to pull up short when a cluster of turquoise mushrooms at the base of an ash tree caught my eye. Mushrooms weren't something Mother ever used for healing, which left me unsure what sort these were. But, similar to the first time I'd used nightbalm berries, I knew I needed these. My magic strained inside me, begging me to do as it bid, the same as it had last time, only then I hadn't recognized it. The mushrooms would help Jax. I wasn't sure how, but I would figure that out once I was back at the cottage.

I harvested twenty, adding them to the growing pile in the scoop of my shirt before continuing my dash back to the cottage.

I burst through the door and stood in the hallway between the two rooms, surveying my three patients. They were all as I'd left them; Willow and Fergus lying on their stomachs, eyes closed, Jax propped against the wall.

Jax watched me through heavy lids. "Can you help them?" His voice was weak.

I nodded, though I wasn't sure. Using night-balm made me queasy. All my life I'd known it as nothing but poison. I could only hope last time hadn't been a fluke.

I checked on Willow. Her chest rose and fell in a steady motion. She'd be fine a few moments longer. I turned to go to Fergus, but as I walked past Jax, his hand shot out, catching my ankle. His grip was loose, I could have kicked it off without raising a sweat. I looked down on him. "I'm helping Fergus first." My voice was hard.

"As you should."

I moved away. If he thought I needed his consent, he was sadly mistaken.

His grip tightened. "Use your magic."

I shook my head, pulling out of his grasp. There was no way I was doing that. "You want me to kill them?"

"Not like that." His voice was weak, just a little more than a whisper.

I wasn't sure if Jax was aware of what he was saying, because sure as the stars, it made no sense to me. "Believe me, if I thought there was another way, I would take it." It would be a thousand times easier with a higher chance of success if I could do what Fergus and Willow did, and wave my hands over their wounds to make everyone better. I didn't have that luxury, and Jax knew it. Or should have, if he weren't so out of it.

As I walked into the bedroom I'd left Fergus in, Jax called, "There is another way. You found it last time."

Fergus was spread out on his stomach, exactly as I'd left him, except that at some point, he'd removed his shirt. It lay in a ball on the floor. His back shone with sweat in the moonlight.

I approached the bed, apprehension prickling my skin. I had to help him survive.

I sat on the edge of the bed and unrolled my shirt and placed the berries, dalliagrass and mushrooms in separate piles beside Fergus. Taking one of the nightbalm berries, I removed the skin and placed a drop of the juice on Fergus' lips, a wisp of my magic surrounding it. Then I waited.

It was the exact thing I'd done last time. Only this time, it was different. Or perhaps it was just that this time, I was searching for the difference.

With no warning, a thread of magenta magic appeared across the top of each of the eight wounds on Fergus' back. It was my magic, no question. But I hadn't called on it. At least, not in the same way I'd accessed my magic in the past.

Each of the threads burrowed down into Fergus' wounds. Fergus shifted on the bed, a groan of pain escaping his lips.

I jumped to my feet, horrified. My magic was burrowing into his body and hurting him. I must have done something wrong. Maybe Jax could tell me how to make it stop.

Before I could ask him, a strand of my magic reappeared from one of the wounds, wrapped around a thick snake-like shaft of red magic. The thin thread rose above Fergus' back, pulling until the thicker magic was fully outside Fergus' body, then my thread of magic wound tighter around the red magic, squeezing until it stopped thrashing, then squeezing again until the red magic disintegrated.

As I stood in the center of the room, my mouth open, the same thing happened from each of his other wounds. Each time Rhiannon's magic disappeared, it seemed Fergus' body relaxed a little more.

I didn't know how I hadn't seen this the last time, except, I guess, I hadn't been watching for it. I'd been so new to magic then, I hadn't even known I could see magic in action.

Healing this way felt different from the other times I'd used my magic. Those times, my body had warmed, and the magic had exploded out of me in a way I hadn't anticipated. Now that I realized what my magic was doing, I could feel it like an extension of my body. The tips of my fingers tingled as the magic removed the infection from Fergus' body and I felt light, happy. It was the same buzz I always got when I saw a patient who'd been gravely unwell make a full recovery. I'd always put it down to happiness at a job well done, but perhaps it was something more.

Once all Rhiannon's magic was gone from Fergus' body, my pink magic settled like a sheet over him. Each time he inhaled, it flowed into him, and I could feel it refilling his reserves and healing his wounds.

I couldn't stop the smile coming to my face as I realized I was using my magic. Properly. Like other fae did. And better still, I was doing it in a way that was helpful. I pushed all the strength I could muster into the blanket healing Fergus, my entire body tingling as he took what he needed from me.

Once I was certain Fergus was no longer in danger, I went to Willow and did the same for her before moving onto Jax.

I crouched by his feet. He cracked his eyes open. "You saved them."

I nodded. I was almost certain they would survive.

"You're going to leave me to die." His voice was weak, his skin clammy.

I looked him over. I was still upset with him over the way he'd treated me, but there was no chance the healer in me would ever walk away without healing him. "I'm not. But I can't do what Willow and Fergus can. I don't know how to heal wounds like yours." I rolled his pant leg up.

Jax blew out a breath and I looked up to find a faint smile on his face. "You're kidding, right? I just watched you pull magic from Willow's body. When Willow heals magical wounds, she fixes the skin and the magic that's in a body slowly makes its way out over days or weeks. You're a Dryad." He shook his head. "I didn't think there were many like you left."

I lifted eyebrows. "A what?"

He shook his head as if what he was saying was obvious. "A fae healer. They use herbs, roots, and leaves mixed with their magic. It's said there is nothing a Dryad's magic can't heal."

I smiled tightly. "Nothing like piling the pressure on. You've seen the way my magic usually reacts." But I'd just seen it, too. And it had done what he'd said.

Jax shrugged again. "Just saying what I see."

It was hard to see the damage to his leg in the dim light, but a sickly sweet odor wafted from his wound and his chest rose and fell at an alarming rate. He was perhaps sicker than I'd expected. I passed him some dalliagrass to chew for the pain and picked up one of the little blue mushrooms I'd collected. My hand itched to lay it over Jax's wounds, but nothing in my training with Mother had ever taught me to do such a thing.

"Just do it." Jax's voice was nothing but a whisper. "Your magic is speaking to you, right?"

I nodded. It wasn't speaking with words, but my fingers tingled with the drive to use it.

"Then do what it tells you. Ask your magic combine with the herbs, ask it to enter my body, tell it to heal me."

I wasn't sure if he was joking. "I've never *asked* my magic to do something before."

Jax's smiled was weak. "Of course you have. How else did you heal Fergus and Willow? You wanted them to live and your magic obliged."

I guess that was exactly what had happened. The difference was, I'd used nightbalm before, so I knew what would happen when I gave it to them. "I want you to live too, Jax, if that's what you're worried about." I'd keep reassuring him, if I had to.

"I know you do." His voice was soft. "That's why you haven't given in to your magic yet. You're scared you'll make a mistake and kill me." He shook his head. "You can't do anything worse than what's going to happen to me if I can't get help."

Jax was dying. There was nothing to lose. Without thinking on it any further, I placed three mushrooms over the center of the wound on his leg.

Jax sucked in a deep breath and his body spasmed. He slid sideways to lie on the ground, letting out a deep groan.

I moved to swipe the mushrooms away.

"Leave them." Jax spoke between gritted teeth. "It's working."

It was. Magenta magic, my magic that had caused the wound, poured from Jax's skin like running water. When it hit the floor, it disappeared into nothing. As the magic left his body, Jax's breathing slowed and the wound healed.

I was still watching the last of the magic run away when Jax sat up and whispered. "Thank you. I didn't deserve your help."

I got to my feet. I needed to check on Fergus, and I wasn't ready for a heart-to-heart. We'd both done things we were ashamed of. "You're welcome."

"I just wanted them back," he whispered. "You understand, right?"

I sighed. "I understand the wanting, not your actions. If someone had told me the only way to get them back was by giving you to the queen, I'd have found another way." He'd treated me more like the enemy than a friend, and it hurt.

Jax gave a single nod, his eyes shining in the dim light. "I was doing the best I could." He shook his head. "The king spent too long in negotiations with the queen. All they did was talk—there was never any action because neither wanted to give the other an advantage. I couldn't leave Fergus and Willow rotting beneath her castle a moment longer, so I sent word to Rhiannon that the king had agreed to a swap on her terms, and went to meet her. The only thing my magic is good for is changing the way things look. And seeing through glamours, although apparently, I'm not even good at that anymore."

Suddenly his need to keep me running along beside Flame yesterday made sense. "You disguised me?"

He nodded. "You were a horse. I was a traveler, off to find somewhere else to live. That's how we got so far. There was no way the king was going to let either of us walk out of his castle together."

I shook my head. "But ... I didn't see your magic. I didn't see myself looking that way."

He gave a faint smile. "Like I said, the only thing my magic is good for is hiding things."

"Who did you use in my place?" Who was it that died on the bridge at Rhiannon's hand?

Jax licked his lips. "Just some fae I met on the trail. I promised she'd be safe, and I'd pay her well."

I stared at Jax, my mouth hanging open. That fae had never been safe.

"I didn't expect her to die. I thought Rhiannon would let her go once she realized I'd tricked her, once I already had Willow and Ferg safely on this side of the river. I thought the queen would hold on to her anger about that until the next time she saw me." Jax's eyebrows were pulled together, his face distraught. "I will visit the girl's family. Take them some gold, not that gold will help with their grief." He shook his head. "I did some terrible things to get Willow and Fergus back, Bria. I'm sorry I was going to swap you for them. It was nothing personal, and it was the only idea I could come up with."

He'd been desperate, the same as I'd been when I hurt him as I escaped. The two of us had been lucky. The rescue had worked out. Besides, I understood his desperation. I understood being backed up against a wall and out of options. Jax wasn't my enemy. "I'm sorry for hurting you, too."

He nodded and closed his eyes, his head dropping back against the wall. "Then I guess we're even."

I started out the door to check on Fergus, turning back to agree. "I guess so."

I crossed the hallway and stood at the door to the bedroom, watching Fergus breathe for a while before heading outside. I was bone weary, but the house was freezing. Before I could sleep, I needed to find some wood for the hearth.

I pulled open the door to find Willow already outside. She sat on the edge of the verandah, staring out across the overgrown yard into the darkness of the forest. Moonlight shone off her blonde hair, and moving shadows from the wind in the trees danced across her skin.

She turned when she heard me and smiled. "Since you're the only other person in the house who's upright, I guess I have you to thank for my current state of consciousness?"

I nodded. "How do you feel?"

"Better than a thousand pieces of gold."

I smiled. "You recovered faster than Fergus." It was a question hidden as a statement. I'd helped Fergus first, yet he still showed no sign of the complete recovery she seemed to have made.

"The queen bound his magic with more suppressors than me. And I suspect he used more of his magic just by bringing us here. He'll be fine, I'm sure. Just give him a little more time."

I hoped so. I couldn't do anything else for him. Time was all we had left.

She sighed, leaning back on her hands and looking up through the foliage to the stars. "It's been so long since I've seen the night sky that I couldn't stay inside a moment longer."

I felt the same way about being outside after so many months stuck indoors, although the events of the last two days had almost cured me of that wish. "I'll leave you alone then. I was just going in search of firewood." She probably wanted time to enjoy it alone.

She shook her head. "Nonsense. Come and sit with me. Tell me how my father treated you."

I crept across the veranda to where she sat, wary of the rotted boards.

Willow frowned. "What are you doing?"

"Trying not to bury my foot beneath the house." I kept my eyes on the ground, hoping I could spot the rotten wood in the dim light.

"Oh." She blinked. "Yes, of course." Yellow magic appeared around her and she flicked her hand, sending a blanket of yellow magic toward the cottage. In the blink of an eye, the cottage went from dilapidated to stunning. The verandah timber became newly stained, and two wooden rockers sat where the rotted boards had been. The front door straightened on its hinges, and the cracked and peeling weatherboards morphed into a newly painted white sheen that glowed in the moonlight. In the garden, the overgrown weeds became a lush lawn, surrounded by a garden overflowing with flowers with a stone fence separating it from the rest of the forest.

I blinked in case I was seeing things. "What just happened?"

A smile split her face. "This is my version of Lanwick Island, my gift from Mother. It's hidden by wards so no one stumbles over it, and in case that doesn't work, I glamoured the house so no one would want to come in if the wards failed." Her smile grew wry. "I guess I forgot you couldn't see the house the way I do. Also, you need not look for firewood. I've set and started the fires."

I couldn't believe what I was seeing. It was a tiny oasis amongst the rugged forest. Two small creatures with glowing wings like a butterfly's chased each other around the flowers. "What are they?"

Willow's smile was lazy. "Garden sprites. They keep the garden tidy and live here because they prefer it to Faery. They're stunning to watch, aren't they?"

I nodded. "You told Raven to bring us here?" She'd turned her head to speak to me as we rode. I hadn't heard her, but perhaps Raven had.

She nodded. "I could not let you go back to Seelie when none of us could talk to Father on your behalf—you'd be dead by now. Jax told me yesterday that Father thinks you escaped, and that he knows nothing about your plot to save Ferg and me."

My smile was tight. It was easier to agree than to explain the lengths Jax had taken to bring them home. "I'm sure your father's not my biggest fan."

"Did he treat you all right?"

I nodded. In that respect, I'd been lucky. I might have spent these past months bored and lonely, but I'd been fed and clothed and treated better than a prisoner.

"I'm glad." We sat in silence before Willow said, "I come to this cottage when I need to think, or when life at the castle becomes too much. It's close enough to the border that I could stay for weeks without my magic growing much weaker, but far enough away that I can relax and be myself. This is where I was coming from the night of the masquerade when I met you at the Crossing."

I started to ask why she hadn't returned to Unseelie through the gap in the border we'd crept through to get here until I realized she rarely traveled by flying horse, and the hole in the border was too high to reach without one.

"Fergus didn't know about this place." She shook her head. "I should have told him, after all, he lets me come and go from Lanwick as I please. I just thought..." She shook her head. "I thought I'd lose my privacy if he found out, that he'd want to come here, the way I sometimes go to Lanwick. There's not much that I can truly call my own in my life, but this cottage is one of those things." She gave me a sidelong glance. "I now realize it was stupid to keep it from him."

I understood the need to hold on to the things that made you feel sane. For me, that thing was healing. "He'll understand." I squeezed her arm. "If he wakes up." I was worried about that. The remedies I'd used since going to Faery were so far removed from what I normally used that part of me expected they would stop working, even as the rest of me knew there was no reason for that to happen.

The door clicked open behind us and I turned to see Jax stick his head out. "Is this a private party or can anyone join in?" He hobbled across the verandah toward us.

I got to my feet, running my eyes over his wound in the dull light. He still had his pant leg rolled up, but the open wound was all but healed. "Are you feeling better?"

He nodded. "Much. Don't leave on my account."

I wasn't. Not really. I swallowed a yawn. "Didn't get much sleep last night." I hadn't slept because I'd been hiding from him. Jax looked at his feet. I guess he knew it. "I'll leave you two alone. Goodnight."

The inside of the cottage had undergone a transformation as amazing as the outside. Dimmed lights twinkled from high on the walls. The dust and dirt were gone, replaced by polished wooden floors. That staircase I'd expected to see when I first walked inside wound up to a second level that hadn't been there before, and more doors than I could count led off the entry hall.

The room where I'd left Fergus had doubled in size, and the bed now sat in the center of the room rather than pushed up against a corner. There was a dressing table beside the door and a rug so plush that it swallowed my feet. Fergus lay sprawled on top of a white duvet which was now a dirty brown beneath his unwashed body. If I'd known what I was laying him on, I'd have found some towels to place beneath him.

He'd rolled onto his back. I sat on the edge of the bed, wishing he would roll back over so I could check his wounds. The movement of the bed disturbed him, and he opened his eyes. "Hi," he whispered, a slow but tired smile coming to his face.

Never had a single word sounded so good. I smiled down at him, certain my relief might break my cheeks. "How are you feeling?"

He closed his eyes and took a deep breath before answering. "Like I might have used a fraction too much magic." His eyes cracked open as he waited for my reaction.

"You think?"

His lazy smile grew wider. He probably still needed to rest, but didn't seem to be in the pain he was in earlier. "Calculated risk."

"Really?" I asked, dryly. "How so?"

"Knew you'd save me." The shadow of a grin remained on his face.

"You trusted my skill that much?" Because I certainly didn't.

He shook his head, his grin growing. "Knew you couldn't bear to be without me, so you'd do everything possible to stop me dying."

I tried to keep my smile from growing. It was good to be sitting beside him again, talking to him. There had been plenty of times over these past months when I wondered if I'd see him again. I gave his arm a gentle punch. "Someone's full of himself given how close he came to dying, and how long it's been since he saw me."

"There's also the fact that you've had months to think about how long I was aware of our bond without telling you." His tone grew heavier and his grin faded.

"There's that, too." It was one thing I wanted to talk to him about once he was better.

"Want to quiz me now?"

I shook my head. Not because I didn't want his answer, but because I was too tired for such a serious conversation. "I think I might head to bed."

Fergus' eyelids were drooping. He patted the space beside him—the part he hadn't dirtied.

I shook my head. Our relationship didn't involve shared sleeping spaces.

"It's just sleep, Bri. Nothing else."

I stilled. "Did you just call me Bri?"

He nodded, eyes closed. "Shouldn't I have?"

I stared at him a moment longer before I made my decision and climbed over him to the empty space. My eyes closed by the time I touched the pillow. "No. I like it, but no one's called me that for years. My father used to use it."

I awoke to movement on the bed and Fergus' voice. "What's wrong with your shoulder, Bria?"

Bright sunlight poured into the room and Fergus knelt on the bed, staring down at me. "Got hit by magic," I murmured, still half asleep.

"And you didn't think to mention it?"

I sat up and sucked in a breath as the wound on my shoulder erupted in agony. My hands were torn up from the suppressors and ached every time I moved, and my muscles were sore and tired from all the exercise I'd had these past two days after months without. I'd been so tired when I fell into bed last night that I'd barely noticed any of it. "Who should I have told? There was no one well enough to help me." Not entirely true. Willow probably could have helped when I saw her outside. "It's not even that bad."

"Have you seen it?" Blue magic swirled around him as he readied himself to heal me.

I put my hand up to stop him. "Do not do that."

"Someone has to. You're dying." His lips were pinched.

I didn't feel like I was dying. "I don't want to go searching for nightbalm berries in the middle of the night again because you don't know when to save your magic."

He sighed and ran a hand through his black hair, nodding. "You're right. Using so much magic yesterday was stupid of me and I'm sorry I worried you." He got off the bed. "Have you seen it? The wound?"

I shook my head. There'd been no chance for that.

He padded over to the dresser and picked up a hand mirror. When he came back, he angled it so I could see.

I drew in a breath. Although the wound hurt, it looked even worse. Through my ripped shirt, my skin was like Jax's had been; red, angry and like something was eating it. "I need some blue mushrooms. They grow beside an ash tree near here." I swung my legs over the side of the bed and pushed to my feet.

The next thing I knew Fergus was lowering me back down onto the bed, his face inches from mine. My heart skipped and my breath caught, the magic of our bond reminding my body what we were supposed to mean to each other. I blinked the feelings away. "What happened?"

"Don't pretend like you didn't faint on purpose just to feel my arms around you." Fergus' voice was light, but he hadn't bothered to cover the concern in his eyes, either because he didn't think I would notice, or because he couldn't. Both options were troubling. More so because I didn't feel as ill as he was suggesting I might be.

His arms, though an unexpected bonus, were the farthest thing from my mind. "I fainted?" I'd never fainted in my life. I sat up, wanting to do nothing but lie down and go back to sleep. "I need the mushrooms."

Fergus shook his head. "It's not possible to heal yourself. Our magic doesn't work that way."

I closed my eyes, trying to ignore the panic rising inside me. When I looked at Jax last night, I thought he was going to die from his wound. Mine looked the same as his had. Maybe worse. I wasn't ready to die.

"Let me heal you," Fergus said, his voice soft. The bed moved as he sat beside me. "I promise I'm well enough."

I opened my eyes and looked him over. Color had returned to his cheeks since yesterday, and his eyes were bright. He moved across the room with the power and grace of a fae prince, and he looked well. But he'd had three months in Rhiannon's dungeon prison. With four suppressors in his shoulders. I didn't want to ask him to use his magic if it would make him sick again.

He gave me a sideways glance. "You let me use my magic on you after you last healed me."

I shook my head. But I had let him. He'd fixed my hands, then we'd danced in the clouds together. Every part of that moment had been possible because of his magic.

A frown creased his forehead, and he stood. "Unless you'd prefer I get my sister to do it?"

I shook my head and took his wrist before he could move away. "I want you to do it."

He smiled and sat down on the bed beside me.

FIVE

"I'M NOT GOING back to Unseelie." Fergus shoveled roast chicken into his mouth like it had been months since he'd seen food. It probably had been. Food this tasty, anyway.

Not only did Willow's cottage have garden sprites, but she had nymphs and brownies living inside the cottage walls, keeping house—tiny winged creatures so beautiful it was difficult to stop looking at them. We'd all slept for most of the day. When I got up, I tried to help cook our dinner, but they shooed me out of the kitchen and wouldn't even allow me to help bring the prepared food to the table. They seemed so pleased to have guests that there was no chance of us finishing all the food they'd prepared, though we were certainly giving it our best shot.

The four of us sat across the end of a large and ornate wooden dining table. My place was set with more cutlery than we owned in our cottage and a napkin made of such heavy fabric, I could have used it to keep myself warm at night. Enormous windows that looked out over the stunning gardens lined an entire wall of the dining room. The windows were thrown open wide, allowing sweet spring air to waft inside until it seemed as if we were eating outdoors.

Willow laughed in response to Fergus' statement, a sound that made me want to smile. She didn't seem to be suffering any ill-effects from her months in Seelie. "Don't be silly."

Fergus shook his head. "I'm not. I hate my life in Unseelie, and Father hates me. He'd prefer if I were dead and he could hold a melee to find the next king."

"That's not true." Willow touched Fergus' arm, her voice softening. "He loves you and he's trying to make you into the best king you can be."

Fergus blew out a rough breath, his nostrils flaring. "I don't even want that job. The life I live at Lanwick is all I need."

I watched their conversation, a piece of broccoli halfway to my mouth. "What if you're exactly what Unseelie needs?"

Jax's eyebrows rose, and he looked at me from across the table. "You've been to Unseelie. What part of Fergus do you think the kingdom needs?"

I lifted my shoulders, feeling stupid. This wasn't my conversation to enter. Unseelie wasn't my kingdom and never would be. But Fergus had more to offer than any of them seemed to realize. "His compassion."

Willow and Jax burst out laughing, the sound harsh in the air.

"What?" My cheeks heated, and I put my knife and fork down before speaking again. "Fergus is very compassionate."

"That's one word for it." Jax's voice was dry, suggesting things about Fergus' and my relationship that weren't true.

Willow grinned at Jax's comment, her smile disappearing as she looked my way. "I'm not sure compassion and Unseelie have ever been used in the same sentence before."

Ignoring Jax, I pushed my point. "Well, maybe they should be."

Fergus shook his head, his unbound black hair flicking across his face. "It doesn't matter. I'm not going back. Ever." He shoved a forkful of carrots into his mouth, his movements defiant.

Jax clicked his tongue. His fork was halfway to his mouth, and he looked like he was deciding whether to speak or eat.

Fergus must have thought the same. "Spit it out, Jax."

Jax licked his lips. The color of his hair seemed to change each time I saw him. Today it was green, just a shade or two darker than his magic. "You are kidding. Right?"

Fergus shook his head. "I'm done with being the king's punching bag." Fergus' hands were tight on his cutlery and his voice strained, but his eyes were down and he stared at his plate.

Jax kept his voice low. "You know you could make him stop."

Fergus' gaze shifted to Jax. His tone was soft, dangerous. "If that were true—and it's probably not—doing so would expose the Wild Hunt."

"But if you are stronger than the king, would it matter?" Jax pushed.

With deliberate movements, Fergus rested his knife on the side of his plate. "Not at all. If I were stronger than him."

"You were once. When you fought back."

I glanced at Willow. She watched the conversation without moving her head, her eyes bouncing from one to the other. Fergus had told me he had once stopped the king hurting him by turning the king's power back on himself. He felt like it was a fluke, like he couldn't do it again. I didn't think he'd tried to stop the king since that day, too concerned with what it might mean for others should he be unable to beat his father.

"Years of pent up rage will do that. It was luck. Nothing more." Tight lines formed around Fergus' lips.

"Now you have an advantage." Jax's eyes moved to me.

Fergus' fork clattered against his plate. "No. I'm not using my bond with Bria in a war against my father. It's dangerous for her and Unseelie is not her kingdom to fight for."

"I'm happy to help any way I can." The words slipped out before I could stop them, but as I spoke, I realized it was true. I would help Fergus however he needed. I just wasn't sure I could actually be of assistance. "Remember though, my magic has a mind of its own." Unless I was using it to heal someone. Then it seemed less ... combustible.

Jax's gaze returned to his friend. "You can't walk out on your duty, Ferg."

"Watch me. I don't care a scrap about my duty." Fergus' jaw worked and he balled his hands into fists that he rested beside his plate. "It's obvious Willow would make a better king than me if there wasn't some archaic rule not allowing women to inherit the throne."

Willow caught my eye and put a finger to her lips, asking me to let the boys sort this out, which I was more than happy to do.

Jax leaned forward in his seat. "We're not talking about Willow, and I think you do care about Unseelie. What will happen if you don't go back?"

Fergus licked his lips. "I live in bliss on Lanwick, see Father once or twice a month as Xion of the Wild Hunt, and I don't have to take part in any ridiculous Unseelie parties for the rest of my life."

Jax lifted a shoulder. "You might be right. I mean, Lanwick is certainly remote enough to miss the fallout. But once your father discovers Rhiannon doesn't have you locked up in her prison any longer, and when you don't return home, what's he going to think?"

Willow sucked in a breath of air. She'd figured it out while I was still waiting to catch up.

Fergus lifted his chin, his lips pressed tight.

Jax pointed a finger across the table at Fergus. "He'll think you're dead." He cast a glance at Willow. "And if you don't go back either, he'll think you are both dead. And then what will he do?"

Fergus' shoulders drooped as he heard what Jax was saying. He mumbled into his chest. "Go to war."

Jax nodded. "Yes, he'll go to war. Proper war. Not the skirmishes at the border that have been going on for years, but full on kill-anyone-who-gets-in-the-way war. You know he has the men. The Wild Hunt has been collecting pawns for his army for years. He'll decimate all of Faery to prove he's stronger than the woman who killed his children. And we all know Rhiannon won't give up easily." Jax's chin rose. "Tell me I'm wrong."

There was silence around the table, punctuated only by the birdsong in the forest.

From what I knew of the king, Jax was right. Fergus knew it, too, though he didn't seem ready to run back to Unseelie yet. "So, I just go back and take all he throws at me?" His voice was like a sharpened blade.

Jax had the good sense not to answer. None of us answered.

Fergus didn't want to hear it, anyway. He shook his head. "I won't go. And I'm not talking about it anymore." He picked up his knife and fork again, roughly cutting a potato and shoving it into his mouth.

The rest of us bent our heads and focused on our meals, though the food didn't taste so sweet as it had before.

It was Fergus who broke the silence, still upset with Jax and looking for someone to take it out on. "So, Willow, you didn't think you should mention you'd received a gift from Mother's estate? I mean, you've known about Lanwick almost as long as I have, and you've spent plenty of time there." The accusation was clear in his voice.

I glanced between them both. I could understand why Fergus might be annoyed Willow hadn't told him about her house here in the woods of Iadrun, but it was perhaps something to ask her in private. Or at the very least, not straight after his best friend had just annoyed the heck out of him.

"You would have told me not to come here!" A little pink circle appeared on each of Willow's cheeks. "You would have said Iadrun is too dangerous for a fae princess to go without protection."

"Because it's true!" Fergus banged his fists on the table, causing the plates and bowls to rattle. "Anyone could find you here, and no one in Faery would even know where to look if you didn't come home." It seemed clear Fergus meant *he* wouldn't know where to search for her.

"Someone was always aware of where I was." Her voice softened, but her face was still hard with anger.

Fergus' eyebrows lifted. Whatever he'd been about to say seemed stolen from his lips. His mouth hung open. "You told someone else about this place?"

Willow nodded.

"She told me," said Jax. "I come here with her sometimes." I got the feeling he wanted to add *for protection* for Fergus' benefit, but didn't dare let Willow know he thought she needed his help.

I suddenly felt like an intruder, listening to a conversation that didn't concern me. I put my cutlery down and stood up. "I'm going to take a walk."

Fergus shook his head. "No need. Sit down. Finish your meal." He looked at his friend, continuing the conversation as if I hadn't spoken. "How lovely. So, are you two dating?"

I sank back down into my seat.

Willow and Jax looked at each other and shook their heads. I was still trying to work out if they were telling the truth or not when Willow got to her feet, crossing the room to pull something from a drawer in the sideboard. She returned and placed it on the table in front of Fergus. "Mother brought you here once." She shook her head, sudden tears pooling in her eyes. "Never me."

Fergus looked down at the paper she'd laid in front of him and his breath hitched. I glanced at

Willow for an explanation, but her eyes were fixed on Fergus.

He pushed the paper along the table to me, using his index finger.

It wasn't paper at all, but a tiny painting. Fergus as a small child, black hair curling around his face and a smile on his lips I would recognize anywhere. He sat on the verandah of the cottage atop a fluffy rug. But it wasn't the picture of himself that caught my attention. It was the woman behind him.

Mother.

Laughing and holding a baby to her chest. Holding me to her chest.

"This was where they brought us?" The one time our mothers had met up after having children, they'd brought us here. I didn't need him to confirm it. Mother in the picture was all the evidence I needed. But Fergus nodded anyway.

This was the place I'd first met Fergus. The place the magical bond between us had started to grow.

No wonder I'd expected to see a staircase in the entry hall when I first walked in. A little part of me remembered this place, even though I should have been too young to recall anything about it. I reached out and squeezed Fergus' forearm before speaking to Willow. "Thank you. For allowing us to come here. And for showing us how much this place meant to your mother."

Fergus nodded. He let out a breath and the muscles beneath my hand relaxed, his anger leaving his body. I'd have to remember to ask him later how he felt about this. "How much it meant to both our mother's," he breathed.

Everyone went back to eating, and the silence grew loud again. I hated it, so I filled the nothingness with a question I'd wanted to ask since the moment I pulled Willow from the river. "Was my mother with you in the Seelie prison?"

Both Willow and Fergus' eyes moved from their plates to me. Willow shook her head.

Fergus said, "We didn't see Aoife after the queen captured us."

"We tried yelling her name while we were down in the prison, but the only answers we ever got were from annoyed Seelie telling us to shut up." Willow's smile was weak.

The news made a little piece of my heart shrivel. Mother could be dead for all I knew, and I had no idea where to search for her body. I looked at Jax. He was pushing food around his plate. "And you haven't heard where she might be?" I'd already asked Jax this, but I had to check again. He hadn't been honest with me about a lot of things the day he broke me out of the castle. Perhaps this was one of them.

He licked his lips. "There have been rumors."

I stilled. "What sort of rumors?" He hadn't mentioned those the last time I asked.

"Rumors that the queen has suddenly grown more powerful." Jax put his knife and fork across his plate, finished with his meal even though there was still a pile of uneaten food upon his plate.

I glanced at Fergus to see if this made sense to him, but his forehead was furrowed. "Do you mean my aunt's magic has grown stronger?" I asked.

Jax nodded.

"How would she suddenly grow more magic?" I was the first to admit there was plenty about Faery I didn't understand, but I was certain that magic was like an arm or a leg; you got what you were born with, and that was it.

Jax shrugged. "I don't know. I'm not even sure it's true. But..."

"But what?" Fergus leaned forward, his forehead still creased.

"The king was delaying your rescue for a reason. Perhaps because he fears her?"

Willow laughed. "Come on, Jax. You don't believe that. Father is not scared of the Seelie Queen."

Jax shook his head. "I've had plenty of time to consider it, and I can only come up with two reasons he left you both rotting in Rhiannon's prison for months on end without even a hint of a tantrum at not getting his way in negotiations with her. And him fearing her is one of them."

Willow and Fergus grew quiet, but I was concerned with something else. "What does this have to do with Mother?"

Jax's eyes widened, like he'd forgotten about me. Or about Mother. "Oh. Well ... there are rumors that your mother has taken her throne back. Or that she's ruling beside Rhiannon, their power combined."

My mouth dropped open. There was no way the woman I knew would do such a thing. But she'd kept so much of her life a secret I wondered if the person I'd grown up with was anything like the Aoife Ridgewing who'd spent most of her life living in Faery. Still, I shook my head. "Mother wouldn't..."

"How is that even possible?" Willow's face carried the same furrowed brow as Fergus'. "The only time magic can combine is with a bonded mate. And they can't be that if they're sisters."

Jax shook his head. "I don't know. I'm just repeating rumors. I have no idea if they're true."

"The royal sword." Fergus spoke quietly, his eyes still on his plate.

Willow shook her head. "That's not true. It's just a child's story." But the shock on her face suggested she believed it was more than a child's story.

"What is the royal sword?" This entire conversation had gotten away from me. I needed one of them to tell me what they were talking about.

Fergus pushed to his feet, walking over to look out the windows. "For many years we've heard rumors that the queen has been searching for a talisman that only the Seelie ruler can use, which would double or triple the power of her magic. No one really believed such a thing existed. What if it does? What if she recently found it and began accessing the power?"

I dragged a hand down my face. An even more powerful Rhiannon was the last thing I wanted to hear about. "And this talisman is a sword, I'm guessing?"

Fergus shrugged. "No one really knows. Over the years, I've heard it referred to as a sword, a dagger, even as a shoe. We don't even know for sure it exists. It's just a rumor."

Willow held up one hand, barely listening to Fergus' explanation. "What if Rhiannon has the sword, or whatever the talisman is, but can't access the power because she's not the real queen? What if, now that Aoife has returned to Faery, Aoife is accessing it because she should be queen?"

I shook my head. She was suggesting Mother had teamed up with Rhiannon, that she would use her power combined with that of the talisman to do Rhiannon's bidding. "Mother wouldn't. Not willingly, anyway." Neither Fergus nor Willow met my eyes. They might not agree with me, but they didn't know Mother like I did. I shook my head. "It's not possible."

Jax shifted in his chair, the only one of the three who would look at me. "I believe the king may agree with you."

My mouth fell open. "Agree with ... me?" The king was the last person I expected to concur with me about anything.

He nodded, his glance dropping to his plate. "Earlier, I said I could come up with two likely reasons that talks between the two kingdoms have gone on so long with little resolution. He's either scared of Rhiannon—"

"He's not." Willow turned her lips down and folded her arms over her chest.

"Or he hoped not only to rescue his children from the Seelie Queen but also wanted to rescue Princess Aoife."

My mouth dropped farther open. The king and I agreed on something? And he was going to find Mother and release her? Perhaps I needed to reassess my opinion of the man.

"That would be very foolhardy of him." Fergus turned to face us, sitting on the edge of the windowsill.

I got to my feet. "Hardly. If Mother needs help, then King Aengus is best placed to give it."

"By opening up our kingdom to someone potentially more powerful than himself? I don't think so." Willow shook her head.

Fergus stretched his feet out in front of him. "I agree with Willow. If there really is a royal talisman, and if Aoife has accessed the magic from it, she may now have more magic than Father. He will not allow someone more powerful than himself to walk into his kingdom."

I walked around the table until I stood in front of Fergus. "He's already done that." My breath caught as his eyes ran over my face. Sometimes—like now, as he looked at me with eyes so intense my heart stopped beating—I forgot he was Prince Fergus Blackwood, future ruler of the Kingdom of Unseelie.

"I don't think so," he said.

He was wrong. "The king kept me alive these past three months. He even treated me well enough. He has no reason to believe you and I will not act on our bond, and we've already shown him that together we're at least a match for his magic." We'd shown him as much the night of Fergus' naming ceremony.

Fergus stared at me a long moment before pushing to his feet and walking the length of the room. Just before he reached the door, he turned back to us and nodded. "Okay. I'll return to Unseelie." He looked over at Jax, still seated at the table. "But I have no intention of staying. I just want Father to know we are safe, and he need not start a war. And I want to find out what he thinks is happening in Seelie and see if he knows anything about where Princess Aoife might be."

We waited for night to come before leaving Willow's cottage so we could use the horses. Fergus called Obsidian to us from Lanwick Island—to a joyous reunion between the two—as well as bringing in a horse for Willow.

We donned our cloaks, Jax and Willow each strapping a sword around their waists, and flew over top of my cottage before returning to Faery. Had there been lights on or any sign someone was there, we would have stopped to check in case Mother was there. Unfortunately, no one had been in the cottage for weeks—the windows were grimy and long weeds grew from the garden—so we continued on to Faery without stopping.

The Unseelie castle looked glorious as we flew toward it. The vast structure was dark and imposing, yet light shone from every window. Fog gathered around the bottom of the castle walls, while the moon—huge and bright—cast a dull light across the grounds.

There were guards on the gates, but few people around and, according to Fergus, no one was here from the outlying courts tonight. Down in the great hall there was always entertainment for those who lived here, with drinking and dancing—and I imagined a lot of other things that made me uncomfortable.

The guards didn't look twice at us as we rode through the gates and led the horses into the stables. It was quiet. Barely another soul around.

"Milo?" called Fergus in a loud whisper, searching for the stable hand who'd helped us last time we brought the horses here. When there was no reply, Fergus shook his head. "Strange." He beckoned us forward, and we took the horses into the back of the stables to hide until we were done. Even though there was no one else around, Fergus still glamoured our horses to look less like the magnificent beasts they were and more like the work horses that lived at the castle.

A frown creased his forehead as we walked toward the castle, the gravel path crunching beneath our feet. He glanced at Jax. "Does it seem ... not busy enough around here to you?"

Jax looked left to right. "There's usually more people around, that's for sure."

"Can you check it out? Make sure everything's okay?"

The hair on the back of my neck rose. "Do you think something's wrong?" After all our talk of the queen becoming more powerful, I was on edge. I had no wish to return to her prison, and no wish for my friends to, either.

Fergus shook his head. "No." He sounded far from confident. "I just think something is different. There would usually be people wandering the grounds. I've never known Milo to leave the stables, or for the outdoor lights not to be lit. It would be good to know what was going on."

Jax peeled off. "I'll start with the Great Hall. If anything's wrong, I'll find you, otherwise, I'll see you back at the stables in half an hour."

"Be careful," whispered Willow, watching him leave before taking the lead.

I fell into step beside Fergus, his long strides almost impossible to keep up with. "Are you nervous to see your father?" I was. I hadn't wanted to bring them here when they were hurt yesterday because I thought the king might kill me. Fergus promised it wouldn't happen tonight—especially now he was back to full strength.

He glanced down at me, the frown transforming into a smile and his steps slowing. He shook his head. "I'm less nervous at seeing him than I've been in my entire life. Because you're with me."

His smile made my heart race. I ignored it. It wasn't even real—it resulted from a stupid spell that had decided we should be together. "Do you think he'll tell us anything we want to know?"

Fergus was silent for a few steps, the only sound our crunching feet. "I doubt it. Father rarely shares anything important with me. I can't imagine today will be any different, but it's worth a try."

Anything was worth a try. I needed to find Mother and had no idea where else to start.

We entered the castle through a side entrance, Fergus pulling the door closed behind us with a quiet click. He expected the king to be in his rooms finishing up his work. Though we tiptoed up the stairs and waited, listening on the landings, we saw no one else. The frown returned to Fergus' forehead, and a matching one grew on Willow's. My stomach churned, spurred on by the worry of my companions.

On the top level, we stepped out into the corridor, heads high. We were expecting the king's footman, Chester, to stop us here, and Fergus said to get past the man we must look confident and as if the king had summoned us. I suspected the bruised faces of his children would be enough to show that we'd just arrived and needed to see the king, not to mention the fact that they'd been imprisoned for three months.

The floor rug muffled our footsteps as we started for the king's rooms.

Fergus and Willow exchanged a glance outside the only door on this level before Fergus strode forward and banged his fist against it. The sound echoed around us, but there was no reply from within. He knocked again, his hand hovering above the door handle. I wasn't sure if he expected an answer this time or if he planned to go in no matter what.

A crash from inside the king's rooms made Fergus jump. He turned the handle and burst through the door before the crashing stopped.

The king's rooms were ... not as I expected. The space was double what Fergus had in his large rooms—which *was* expected. What I hadn't anticipated was how untidy these rooms would be. Dresser drawers sat open with under-clothing hanging haphazard over the edges. Tunics and pants lay scattered across the floor and the bedding was pulled back as if the king had just thrown off his covers a moment ago.

Fergus cleared his throat. "Father?"

It took a second to find the king among the belongings strewn around the room. He was kneeling on the floor, his head low and butt high as he searched for something beneath his bed. He looked up at Fergus' voice, using the bed to push to his feet.

His grey hair was tied back neatly at his neck and his clothing was casual—black pants and a dark grey shirt. The top button of his shirt was open, the sleeves rolled up to his elbows.

"Fergus. Willow." He walked over to Fergus and wrapped his arms around him. Fergus stood for a moment with his hands by his sides, then slowly lifted them and patted his father's back. The king hugged Willow, too. His eyes fell on me, and though he looked me over, he said nothing. To his children, he said, "I'm glad you're here. I need your help."

I pressed my palms together, hurting on behalf of Fergus and Willow. Both of them had been held against their will for three months and when they finally returned, their father couldn't even spare a moment to ask how they were.

Fergus seemed unbothered. "What is going on, Father?"

The king's shoulders rose, then fell. He looked between all of us before taking a step to close the distance. "The queen is trying to kill me. She wants to rule Unseelie."

Fergus glanced at Willow. "How do you know?" It was what we suspected, too, but Fergus was treading carefully around the king, making sure we understood what was going on before revealing what we knew.

The king shook his head. "Isn't it obvious?" He waited for one of us to speak. When no one did, he said, "Did you see any of my staff in the hallways? Was anyone heading into the Great Hall? Did you see anyone at all on your way up here?"

We shook our heads. Fergus had said that was odd. I still wasn't sure what it signaled and didn't think he knew what to make of it, either.

"She's taken them! All of them," the king bellowed.

Willow moved to stand beside her father, placing a hand of his arm. "Taken who? Chester?"

The king nodded, "Yes. Chester."

Willow's frown deepened. "Where would she take him? And how ... and why?"

The king shrugged. "How would I know what that woman's done with him? And don't you think if I knew where he was, I'd go and get him back? But it's not just him. My kitchen staff are gone.

The gardeners, the stable hands. Everyone is gone." The king turned away and crouched beside his bed again.

I wanted to know if the queen had killed his people or kidnapped them, but couldn't bring myself to ask, so instead I stuck with the reason we'd come here. "Have you seen my mother? Aoife Ridgewing? Have you heard from her?"

The king's head swung around to look me over. His smile was saccharine as he climbed to his feet once more. "Aoife. Why, yes. I know where she is."

"Well?" If the frown lines between Fergus' eyes were anything to go by, this conversation was not going the way he expected.

It certainly wasn't what I expected. The two other times I'd seen the king, I'd thought him cunning and astute. Today he seemed flustered and unsure of himself. He didn't even seem that bothered that his staff were missing. He wasn't doing anything about it, that was for sure.

"The queen has her, of course. I can't believe you had to ask." There was a snap to his voice. He made to get down on his knees again, then seemed to think the better of it, turning back to face us. "I can get her back. I was on my way there until you all interrupted.

Fergus' eyes narrowed. "With respect, Father, you were crouched on the floor of your bedroom when we found you. You were going nowhere."

"I was looking for Hellfire. Can't for the life of me recall where I put it." He shook his head as if he were clearing it. "Aoife Ridgewing is being taken against her will into Seelie this night. I'm going to bring her back to Unseelie. I'd welcome your help."

I stepped forward. "The queen is taking my mother into Seelie tonight? From where?"

"Iadrun." He spoke like it should be obvious.

I could have kicked myself. We'd only given a cursory glance to my unlit cottage as we flew past, assuming its darkness meant Mother wasn't there. What if she had been? Maybe she was cowering beneath the cottage with all the lights out, hoping no one would find her.

"But if I don't find my sword, she'll pass the border before I get there." He bent again, searching beneath his bed.

Willow wandered into her father's closet, coming out a moment later with his sword in her hand. "Could it be *this* Hellfire you're searching for, Father?" She grinned at him. The gesture surprised me. From what Fergus had told me, I could never imagine him joking with his father. I guessed the two children had different relationships with the man.

The king smiled back. "There it is. How stupid of me. Of course that's where I left it." He looked between Willow, Fergus and me. "I really could use some help at the border, if anyone has some time for their old man."

Fergus and I stepped forward together. "We'll come," we both said, smiling at each other as we spoke.

The king nodded, looking at Willow.

"I will, too. I'll meet you in the tunnels. Just need to ... do a couple of things." She needed to find Jax and bring him with us. I wasn't sure why she didn't tell her father she was going for extra help.

"Perhaps those things could wait, daughter. Time is of the essence." The king threw his tunic on, then strapped his sword around his waist before rolling the sleeves of his shirt back down to his wrists.

Willow shook her head. "They can't. But I'll be there to fight with you, Father. Don't worry."

The king licked his lips, and I thought he was going to demand Willow's assistance. Instead, he gave a slow nod. "We will see you soon, then."

As Willow ran out the door, the king ushered Fergus and I to the back of his rooms, opening what looked like a cupboard and directing us inside. I glanced at Fergus. He took my hand and leaned over to speak in my ear. "It's okay. It's just another entrance to the tunnels." A way to get us to the border, and to Mother, fast.

I followed Fergus into the dimly lit hallway so narrow I could stretch out my arms and touch the stone walls. My heart hammered as we started for a steep staircase that led down to complete darkness. And, eventually, I hoped, to Mother.

I wasn't sure how the king had gone from enemy to ally, but I was pleased he had. Between us, we could save Mother from whatever the Seelie Queen wanted with her. And it was partly because of Fergus. "Thank you," I whispered.

He opened his mouth to speak but was interrupted by the door to the king's rooms opening so fast it slammed against the stone wall behind it.

"Stop!" Jax raced through the door, Willow at his heels. "Fergus! Don't go with him. That's not your father, it's the queen!"

Fergus, the king and I all turned on the spot and stared at Jax, mouths gaping.

"I can see through her glamour," he pressed. "It's not your Father!" He ran toward us, pulling his sword from the belt beneath his cloak.

He didn't get far. The queen—it was definitely her now, her glamour was gone, and she wore a burgundy dress, her blonde hair spilling down her back—flung out her hand, red magic flying from her fingers.

Willow screamed, throwing a shield around herself and Jax. The blast was still hard enough to knock them both to the ground and push them back across the wooden floor toward the doorway.

Fergus drew a shield around the two of us and a ball of magic appeared in his hand, ready to throw at her. But he wasn't fast enough. The queen pulled a shield around her body, and Fergus let his magic die on his fingertips. Six of the queen's guards in their grey uniforms sprinted into the king's rooms.

The two of us were already through the door and could have run down the stairs into the tunnels and escaped; there was no one in front of us. Once in there, it would be easy to lose a pursuer. But it wasn't an option. Not with Willow and Jax trapped between the queen and her guards.

Fergus cursed under his breath. "Swords it is." His magic flared, and a sword appeared in each hand. He passed one to me.

I shook my head. "You know I can't use this." I'd only held a sword once before, and it had almost been a complete disaster. The stakes seemed even higher now.

He lifted his eyebrows. "Just do your best. And remember who it was that kept you locked in her prison for weeks on end." He raised his sword, eyes on the queen standing in front of us.

He couldn't expect me to use this thing. "Wait! Will your shield protect me if I get this wrong?"

He shook his head, grinning like he was looking forward to what was to come. "That's only for magic. Which we won't be using today."

"Why not?" It seemed an odd time to drop the one advantage we might have.

"Because we've all employed our shields." He started to move.

I threw my hands up. What the heck? We'd all used shields in the ballroom of this very castle, and we'd still used our magic on each other. "That makes no sense."

Fergus waved his sword in a figure eight, a practice maneuver. "Look out there." He pointed through the little cupboard door to the king's rooms. The queen stood between us, staring at Willow and Jax, a red shield around herself. Jax and Willow were surrounded by Willow's yellow shield and behind them, the queen's red shield protected the guards. "It's a magic stalemate. While the queen splits her magic that way, looking after her guards, we're likely all as strong as each other. If we want to win, we're going to have to do this the human way." Fergus stepped around me.

I reached out and gripped his arm, speaking under my breath as I called on my own magic. "What about our magic together—"

Fergus pulled away, dragging his magic with him before it joined with mine. "Don't," he said, through gritted teeth. Before I had time to think about what his reaction might mean, he marched out the little door and brought his sword down toward the queen's neck.

She whirled around to face him and before his weapon got anywhere near her, she blocked his swing with her sword. The clashing of metal rang around the room.

Behind them, Jax jumped to his feet, connecting a wild swing of his sword with a guard's neck. The guard dropped to the ground, blood gushing from this fatal wound.

Willow used her own sword to block a shot from another guard. Every one of them seemed more than proficient with their swords. And then there was me. Standing uselessly in the background, waiting for everyone else to save my life.

No. I wouldn't be that person. I wouldn't just stand here and let them risk their lives while I did nothing. Gripping the hilt of my sword, I crept into the room until I was behind the queen.

I'd tried this method of attack the only other time I'd held a sword. It was the only thing I could think of.

I raised my sword above my head, and, as Fergus fought with the queen, brought it down toward her back. She turned so fast, all I saw was a blur of movement. The next thing I knew, my sword collided with her sword, pain jarring up my arms. My fingers went numb and my sword flew from my grasp, landing with a thud and skidding across the floor and through the door into the tunnels. I shrank backward. No weapon and no way to fight.

The queen advanced on me, her sword shining under the bright light of the king's rooms.

I ducked, closing my eyes and waiting for the impact. It never came.

When I opened my eyes, the queen had turned away and was focused again on Fergus.

I let out my breath. Not dead yet. Not hurt either, though I had a very strong urge to hurl. Coming to Faery had shown me there were a whole new set of skills I needed to master. Like magic. And apparently swordsmanship, too.

I glanced at Willow and Jax. They were outnumbered, two to one, but as I watched, Willow flicked the weapon away from one of her attackers, the same way the queen had just disarmed me. It flew out the other side of him, away from me, too. He was as weaponless as me, and it gave me an idea.

It wasn't often I was at an advantage here in Faery, but I hoped now might be one of those times.

I launched myself at the guard, fists flying. He either didn't see me or didn't expect me to use my fists. I'd been fighting this way since I was a child. I'd had to learn to defend myself against bullies who taunted me over my mutilated ears since I was big enough to walk, and I backed myself in a fist fight. I landed the first blow just beneath his eye, opening up a cut. Before he had the chance to retaliate, I landed an uppercut to his jaw. He crumpled onto the stone floor, out cold.

I ran up to the guard fighting Willow and jumped on his back, clinging on tight with my legs. He tried to throw me off, but his blade was useless at this angle. I wrapped my arms around his neck, cutting off his breath. This was a move I'd never used before in a fight, and I hated that I knew how to stop him breathing because of my training as a healer. Still, it was him or me, and I chose me.

He sank to the ground. I went with him, my arms around his neck until I was sure he wouldn't get up again.

By the time I looked up, Willow and Jax had dispatched the final two guards and were advancing on the Seelie Queen. It was four against one. We could end her here and now.

Jax and Willow raised their weapons, spreading out around the queen.

"It's over, Rhiannon," panted Fergus.

"Oh, it's far from over, Prince." And, with a wave of her hand, the queen disappeared.

The four of us stared at the place the queen stood moments before, and Jax cursed. "Where did she go?"

"Back to Seelie with any luck," Willow puffed.

Jax glanced at the open tunnel door. "We have to get out of here. There are Seelie guards down in the prison, lots of them. If the queen instructs them to come after us, we aren't leaving alive."

Fergus nodded. "This way." He led us through the cupboard door and into the tunnels, and we climbed down a set of stairs so narrow, my shoulders touched each side. Fergus and Jax had to turn sideways to get through. At the bottom of the stairs, we took another two steps, and we were suddenly standing outside the stables.

I turned in a circle, trying to figure out how the tunnels worked. I couldn't even see where we'd come from. "Maybe we should have gone into the castle that way, too."

Fergus shook his head, already striding into the stables. "Can't get into Father's rooms through the tunnels, only out."

I nodded and swallowed back sudden tears as I realized what had just happened. I didn't have to go to the Crossing tonight to know Mother wouldn't be there. The queen had given me hope and then ripped it away. I'd cry later, somewhere more private.

With my chin raised, I followed Fergus into the stables, stopping beside an empty stall when I heard a noise. We didn't need an ambush on our way out of here.

With my fingertips, I pushed the stall door open.

Nothing seemed out of sorts in the dim stall. The water and feed buckets were already filled, awaiting the next equine guest. There was hay in the back corner and the stall was clean. I was about to follow my friends down to Raven when the pile of hay moved.

Someone was there.

I crept forward, wishing again I had learned how to use a sword. If I was carrying one now, I could jab it into the hay and kill the Seelie fae hidden there. I must remember to ask Fergus to teach me.

I stood beside the pile of hay, watching for the movement. The moment I saw it, I reached in and grabbed hold of the Seelie beneath, dragging him out into the open by the front of his shirt and drawing my arm back to hit him.

The man put his hands up in front of his face. "No. Don't hurt me. I didn't do anything." He spoke slowly, his voice quivering.

"Bria! Stop!" Fergus sprinted into the stall behind me. My hand was already moving when I realized the man in front of me wasn't wearing the grey uniform of the Seelie guards. I pulled my punch as Fergus yelled again. "Don't. It's Milo! He's not one of them!"

I let the man go, staggering back, my hands going to my lips. I couldn't make sense of what I was seeing.

Fergus was right when he said that man wasn't one of the Seelie guards. I knew it the moment my eyes landed on his face. But he wasn't Milo. He was someone better.

I ran forward and wrapped my arms around his neck.

"Father! I thought you were dead."

SIX

FATHER pulled out of my grip, shaking his head. He raised his hands in surrender. "I didn't hurt anyone. Just hid."

Fergus stepped between us, placing a firm hand on Father's shoulder. "Milo. It's me. It's Prince Fergus."

Father shook his head, his gaze fixed on the ground, refusing to meet anyone's eyes. "Just hid. No hurting."

Fergus bent into his line of sight, his voice gentle. "Milo. It's me, Fergus. You're safe."

Father blinked, his head slowly lifting. "Prince Fergus. You're alive?" He reached out and touched Fergus' face as if he couldn't believe what he saw. "I thought they killed you all. They said they were going to, so I hid. I didn't hurt anyone. I didn't."

"I know you didn't, Milo. You're safe now." Fergus spoke with extreme gentleness, like he didn't want to spook him.

"This isn't Milo. This is my father. Myles Ridgewing." I stepped up beside Fergus. "Father, it's me, Bria." How was this happening? Father was dead. Fergus had carried him away that night after the Wild Hunt had pumped their magic into him and ended his life. Yet, here he was, living in Fergus' home.

Father's eyes went distant. "Bria. I knew a Bria once. She was beautiful."

My eyes filled with sudden tears. He was alive. He really was. "It's me, Father. I'm Bria."

Father shook his head. "I don't know Bria now." Apart from the pointed ears which I'd never seen on him before, he looked and sounded like the man I knew, except his speech was slow.

I glanced at Fergus. If I couldn't convince Father who I was, perhaps I could convince Fergus. "This is my father. Myles Ridgewing. You must remember him."

Father nodded. "I was Myles once." He sounded wistful.

"You're still Myles." My voice was firm. I needed him to realize it. I reached out to touch his shoulder, but he shrank away, so I dropped my hand.

Father looked past me and into the distance. "Aoife knew Bria, too."

I glanced at Fergus. He shook his head and raised his palms. "I don't understand what is happening here. This is Milo. He's worked for us for years." He shook his head, his fingers pressing against his temples. "But you're right. No matter how hard I try, I can't remember what your father looked like. Why can't I remember him?"

"The spell?" The king had spelled Fergus' memory of that night. He thought he'd broken it, that he'd remembered everything there was to recall about that night, but perhaps the spell was more powerful than he thought.

"I guess so." He nodded.

"Bria and Aoife like the invitation." Milo's face split into a huge grin as he recalled something no one else did.

"Father, have you seen Mother? Have you seen Aoife?" Maybe she traveled to Unseelie with the queen.

He shook his head. The grin disappeared from his face and his eyes filled with sorrow. "Aoife is gone. She left with Bria. A long time ago."

"We can't leave him here." I looked at Fergus. Now I'd found him, I wasn't walking away from him, no matter that he didn't remember me.

Fergus ran a hand down his face. "You're sure this is your father?"

I nodded. Of course, I was sure. How could he even question it?

"I knew a Bria once." Milo retreated to the darkest corner of the stall, the fingers of one hand clasped in the other. "Aoife knew her, too."

"Can he ride?" My father could, but the man cowering in the darkness was a shell of that man. I hoped that working in the stables meant riding wasn't as foreign to him as having a daughter seemed to be.

Fergus nodded. "But he never goes far from the stables. He'll refuse if you try to take him farther."

I shrugged. "I can be convincing."

"He won't leave this place. He never does. It's where he feels safest." Fergus turned his head to the stable door, the horses stomping in the back stalls drawing his attention.

We had to go. Rhiannon's guards would be searching for us. "He can ride on Raven with me."

Fergus nodded. "I'll bring her to you."

I drifted toward Father. I didn't want him scared of me, so I used the name he seemed most comfortable with. "Milo. We're going to leave the castle. Would you like to come with us?"

He shook his head, hard and fast. "Can't leave. Bria might come."

I touched my chest. "I am Bria. I've come for you."

The head shaking grew harder. "No. Everleigh said Bria could fly. Aoife is dead and Bria flies. That's what Everleigh said. Did you find her? Did you find Everleigh?"

I didn't know who Everleigh was, nor did I care at this moment. "I'm Bria. And I can fly. I have a horse—"

"No! I'm not going." His voice was loud, and he stomped one foot before shrinking back into the corner.

I blew out my breath. He could get as angry at me as he liked, but I was not letting him stay here. Hooves clopped along the stable floor toward us. I put my hand out to him. "I can fly, Milo. I have a horse that will take us up into the sky and away from this place."

He shook his head again. "No. Can't leave. Must stay." He took another step away until he'd backed into the corner. "Find Everleigh. She'll tell you."

I sized him up, wondering if I could throw him over my shoulder and drag him onto Raven's back. Unlikely. He was almost as tall as Fergus, and lean. I imagined since he worked with the horses, he was strong, too. I'd have to come up with another way to get him out of here.

Fergus and Raven stopped outside the stall and I pulled the door open so Father could see them both. "See. This is Raven. She can fly and she'll take us away from here."

Father shook his head the moment I began to talk.

I suppressed the groan that wanted to escape my lips and walked over to Fergus. "Why doesn't he like to leave the stables?"

Fergus shrugged. "I don't know. I've tried for years to get him to come onto the grounds with me, or for a ride, but he always refuses."

I turned to look at Father. He stared with longing at Raven. He wasn't scared of riding her, so something else was the problem.

I considered the things I knew about him. The king sent the Wild Hunt to our home, searching for Mother and me. The king gave the Wild Hunt instructions to kill my father once they had the information they required. Although, looking at him standing across the stall, perhaps those instructions had been to bring him to Faery rather than kill him. The king gave Father a home here at the castle and kept him alive.

The king was the common factor in everything.

I looked past Fergus toward the back of the stables. "Is Jax still here?"

Fergus nodded. "He's bringing Flame and Obsidian out now so we can leave."

I sidled past Raven and ran down to Jax.

When I returned to the stall, I stood at the door and held my hand out toward Father. Fergus watched me with a furrowed brow. "Come, Father. We need to leave the castle. King Aengus said we must."

Father's eyes widened. "King Aengus? No. He never comes to the stables."

"He's here now. Come to make sure his loyal subjects make it out of Unseelie before the Seelie Queen attacks." As I spoke, Jax walked up beside me looking so much like King Aengus, it stole my breath. He was dressed in a deep green tunic and black pants, a heavy cloak thrown over his shoulders, and his silver hair was plaited down his back.

Jax cast his eyes around the stall, his chin raised in perfect replication of the king. "Ah, Milo. There you are." Stars. He even sounded like the king.

Milo straightened, then dropped into a low bow. "Y-your Highness."

"I fear you are not safe here at the castle," Jax said. "The Seelie Queen is coming."

"I could fight her, your Highness." He straightened and shook his fist at the thin air.

Jax smiled. "That's a generous offer, but I cannot accept. I believe the safest option for everyone at this time is to leave. I'm going to need you to climb on this horse with Bria. She'll take you away from here."

"And what about you?" Father wrung his hands.

"I'm leaving too." Jax caught my eye, giving his shoulders a shrug like he wasn't sure if he was saying the right thing.

I didn't know either. I was working on the hunch that the king had commanded—or spelled—Father to stay here, and that the command would be broken once Father believed the king told him to leave. If I was wrong, I didn't have another plan.

"What do you say, Milo? Will you get on this horse with Bria?" Jax smiled at Father.

Father nodded and took some uncertain steps toward us. "I knew a Bria once."

Father sat in front of me upon Raven's back on our way to Lanwick Island. I closed my eyes and let Raven go where she needed, content to wrap my arms around Father's waist even if he didn't recognize me.

At Lanwick, I settled him into a guest chamber down the corridor from mine. His eyes almost burst out of his head when he saw the luxurious bed that took up most of his room. He climbed onto it and lay down, and was almost asleep by the time I let myself out the door.

I returned to my room, bathed, changed and slept, but was wide awake before dawn and couldn't return to sleep.

I was desperate for Father to wake so I could try again to make him remember me. I wanted to hear what his life had been like since he left us, why he hadn't come home, and who Everleigh was. But those questions would have to wait until he woke. Considering them myself didn't give me the answers I desired.

I walked out through the sliding door that led to the pool, inhaling the humid air I'd missed so much during the months I was locked in the Unseelie castle. For a few minutes, I sat with my feet dangling in the pool until I realized that I was hoping Fergus might be awake in his rooms and that he'd come and sit with me. Climbing to my feet, I went back inside, walking straight through my room and out the other door into the hallway. I hadn't explored Fergus' mansion. I hadn't explored the island either, but now, while it was still too dark to look around outside, I was going to take the opportunity to check out the inside.

Up the stairs in front of me were Fergus' rooms. I'd been up there once and had no intention of going there now, so I turned left out my door and followed the hallway. Closed doors dotted the corridor on both sides—probably more rooms like mine and Father's. Why did one person need so many rooms?

I heard Fergus' voice inside my head, providing the answer. *Because I'm a prince, of course.* Despite myself, I smiled. As if that was even a reason.

I kept walking until I found an open door. I stuck my head inside and couldn't keep from gasping. It was a music room, filled with every instrument I knew and many I didn't.

A larger version of the outside pianoforte I'd listened to Fergus playing sat in the center of the room, the stool pushed neatly beneath the keys. String instruments lined one wall, hanging from largest to smallest—violin, viola, cello, and another that was similar but larger—while wind instruments hung from the opposite wall. Drums—both hand drums and ones played with sticks—sat in the corner near the string instruments. Couches lined one wall, and chairs were stacked in a corner, like this room could be set up for a concert. I wandered from instrument to instrument, my fingers trailing over each one. Could Fergus play all these? Would he play for me? Or show me how? I'd start with the pianoforte ... no, the violin. Or perhaps I'd learn to sing properly.

I sighed. If I had a room like this in my home, I might never want to leave it.

Voices in the corridor made me jump. One of them was Fergus. The other was a woman whose voice I didn't recognize. They stopped outside the door.

"I could have done it," Fergus said.

I glanced at the couches across the room, weighing up the chances of running across there and hiding behind them in case Fergus and his friend walked in. I stayed glued to the spot, scared that moving would alert them I was here, snooping where no one had allowed me to go.

"No point wasting effort on regret." The female had one of those tinkling voices that sounded as beautiful as I imagined she was.

Fergus laughed. He hadn't laughed once with me these past few days. "Regret is all you're going to get from me this morning." He pushed open the door.

I ducked behind the drum set, watching the two of them from between the drums.

Fergus pulled out the pianoforte stool, sat and played a couple of notes. His friend sat on the couch opposite, kicking her long legs out in front of her. I'd seen her before. She was the girl who'd come into his room when we returned from Seelie and thought Fergus was going to die. And she was just as beautiful as she sounded, with her long black hair, full lips and piercing brown eyes.

Following them into the room and sniffing her way from corner to corner, was Buttercup. I nearly jumped out of my hiding place right then at the sight of her. The last time I'd seen her, she was lying injured on the ground as the queen's guards attacked us in Unseelie, and I assumed she had died that night. It filled my heart to see her alive. I wanted to wrap her up in a hug.

"I've never wanted to do something I shouldn't as much as I did right then," Fergus continued, a trio of notes coming from the pianoforte.

"She did offer..."

One of Fergus' shoulders lifted. "She didn't know what she was offering. She doesn't want this for her life. She doesn't want me."

"Then she's a fool."

He shook his head. "Unlike us, she has choices. And she wants to use them. It's not a crime."

What were they talking about? Me? Or some other nameless she?

Buttercup sniffed the air, then trotted toward the drums. I huddled into a smaller ball, willing her not to give me up. It didn't work. She came around my side of the drums and stopped when she saw me. Then her tail began to wag. I reached out to pat her, hoping Fergus didn't wonder what she was doing back here and come for a look.

Buttercup dropped onto the ground and rolled over, legs up, waiting for a stomach rub. I wasn't sure how I'd ever found her scary.

I reached over and patted her. As she wriggled beneath the pleasure of her stomach rub, her foot hit a stand and a symbol clattered.

"Buttercup. Come out of there." Fergus stood, calling his dog. When she didn't move—big eyes on me waiting for more rubs—he started toward the drums. "Who's there?"

I climbed slowly to my feet. I was caught. "It's only me. Sorry. I shouldn't have come in here." I put my head down and started for the door.

"Bria? I expected you'd be sleeping like everyone else. Come back in here and meet Crystal."

I wasn't sure I was in the mood to meet the beautiful Crystal, but I plastered a smile on my face and turned back to them. "Hi Crystal."

Crystal looked me over from head to foot without returning my smile. "It's nice to properly meet you, Bria. Last time you were here, you left so quickly."

I couldn't tell if there was a bite to her words, if she was upset with me. "Well, I never intended to be here long." And it wasn't like we'd been introduced, so finding her to say goodbye would have been odd.

"And you didn't intend for Fergus to stay, either?" She lifted her eyebrows.

Oh, she was definitely upset. Uncalled for, in my opinion. "You think I forced Fergus to leave the island with me?" As if I could force him to do anything. He'd offered to come and help get Mother out of Unseelie. Everything that happened after that wasn't my fault.

Crystal shrugged.

"Believe me, if I could control Fergus, I would never have *allowed* him to use up all his magic so he almost died." Twice.

Fergus seemed like he was trying not to smile. He'd be better off using that energy to tell Crystal that I hadn't made him do anything.

Crystal stared at me while I tried to read her expression. Surprise? Anger? I wasn't sure. Her face split into a grin. She looked at Fergus. "I like her. She's going to keep you on your toes, Prince."

I shook my head, my own surprise showing at her sudden change in demeanor. "I won't be here long this time, either. Fergus can go back to doing whatever he does just as soon as I've found my mother."

A look passed between the two of them that I couldn't decipher.

"Well, don't rush off on my behalf." She stood and walked over to Fergus, gave him a hug, then started out of the room.

"You're leaving?" called Fergus.

"Things to do, places to be. Don't you two do anything I wouldn't do." Her tinkling laughter followed in her wake.

I watched her walk out the door before turning to Fergus. "Sorry. I didn't mean to eavesdrop. I couldn't sleep, so I went exploring and found this place, and wow, it's amazing..." I was babbling.

Fergus smiled. "It's fine, Bria. You can come in here—or anywhere on the island—any time you like." He sat on the pianoforte stool and began to play.

I watched his hands fly over the keys, each doing something independent of the other. I could never be so coordinated as to do that. The music was fast and jolly, and in complete contrast to the other time I'd heard him play. When he finished, I said, "You're in good spirits."

He swiveled on the seat, smiling up at me. "Am I? Must be the ocean air."

And likely being back home after so long away. "Is she your girlfriend?" Okay, so I wasn't allowing my brain to filter my thoughts before letting them slip from my mouth.

Fergus checked his smile. "Would it bother you if she was?"

I shook my head, but the movement was too soon and too fast, and even I didn't believe myself. When had I started caring who Fergus had in his life?

His grin widened. He didn't believe me, either—no surprises there. He got to his feet. "There's no need to be jealous."

"I'm not jealous. Why would I be jealous? Just because she's beautiful, with legs up to her armpits." Not to mention she was the first person Fergus sought when he arrived home. "You two make the perfect couple."

His lips twitched. "Well, I'm glad we have your blessing."

I couldn't meet his eyes, because if I were honest, they didn't have my blessing. And that was complete selfishness. I didn't want the bond I had with him, so he should be free to see whoever he wanted. I changed the subject. "Last night, Father mentioned someone called Everleigh? Do you know who she is? He told me to find her."

Fergus shook his head, a frown creasing his forehead.

As I recounted the conversation, I suddenly understood where my restlessness came from. "Everleigh told him Aoife was dead and Bria could fly." My voice shook. One part of that sentence was true. I hoped the other part was not.

I didn't realize I was pacing back and forth across the room until Fergus caught my hand and pulled me to a stop. He waited until I raised my eyes to meet his before speaking. "It's okay, Bria. We'll find her."

I nodded, unsure if he meant Mother or Everleigh. Either way, his reassurance was enough to send the bleak thoughts in my head skittering away. We would find Mother. We'd done it once before. But thinking about Mother reminded me of what we'd seen at the castle. "Any word of the king?" It should have been the first thing I asked him, instead of worrying only about myself. Fergus had to be as concerned about his father as I was about Mother.

He shook his head. "There were no bodies lying around the castle, which is a good thing. Jax thinks the guards were congregating in the prison because that's where they are holding the castle staff. And I assume it's also where they're holding Father. The Wild Hunt are only just back from a night in Iadrun. Once they've rested, I'll take them to Unseelie at dusk to check it out and attempt to rescue him."

"And how are you feeling about all this? About your father going missing?" His hand was still gripping mine. I gave it a squeeze.

The frown returned to Fergus' face. "Fine."

I tilted my head, trying to work out what his reaction meant. "Why do you look confused?"

He shook his head. "Not confused. Surprised. No one has asked me about my feelings in relation to Father in a very long time."

"Ah." I nodded, trying to look solemn. He was so serious it would do him good to smile.

The frown that adorned his face grew deeper. "What does that mean?"

"Nothing. It's just makes sense, that's all." I kept my tone light.

He watched me with narrowed eyes, probably trying to work out where this conversation was heading. "It does?"

"At least I understand why you gave such a rubbish answer to my question."

He rewarded me with a smile, then released my hand, going to stand beside the long window that looked out across the beach. "Honestly, Bria, I don't know how I feel. Part of me hopes the queen hasn't hurt him, while another part hopes he feels even a fraction of the pain he's inflicted on me over the years. The selfish part of me hopes he's not dead because I'm not ready to be king, but then, if he dies, part of my life becomes a lot less complicated. And after I think all these things, I feel guilty for thinking them because he's my father and I should want him back alive." He dragged a hand down his face.

I walked over to stand beside him. The sky was bright orange as the first rays of sun hit the beach. "The only thing you shouldn't be feeling is guilt. Everything else is justified."

He let out a harsh laugh. "It might be justified, but it's not the way a son should feel about his father."

I shook my head. "There is no single way you're supposed to feel, and no one should tell you how to feel. They're your feelings and they're born from your experiences with your father."

He watched the ocean in silence before turning to me, a faint smile lighting his face. "I didn't know you were so profound at this hour of the day."

I grinned. "I aim to please."

"You always do." His smile widened, and he straightened his shoulders. "Now, about this Everleigh person. Are you up for some research?"

I nodded. I was up for anything that might help find Mother.

Fergus led me from the music room farther along the hallway where I hadn't explored, and into another wing of his home, taking me into a library. It was, like everything else in Fergus' home, huge with high ceilings and a window running along one wall that looked out over the ocean. Books lined every wall from floor to ceiling, and a rolling ladder sat beneath the racks, making it possible to reach the highest books. The room was meticulously tidy and had a desk with a table lamp upon it in the center of the room.

"You own all these books?"

Fergus nodded. "Mother was the daughter of the Lord of the Winter Court, and her people are the keepers of Unseelie history." Fergus shrugged. "I guess Grandmother didn't expect Mother to marry. She set up the island for her as a refuge." He smiled at the memory of his mother.

"A refuge with books and music." Sounded perfect to me, and I couldn't keep the envy from my voice.

Fergus looked around the room. "I have no clue why she married Father rather than making her life here."

I turned in a circle, my gaze jumping from one book to the next. One day, when all this was over, maybe I could come back here to relax for a day or two. I'd make use of this library, the pool and music room—and that would be within the first day. "Were they bonded?" I didn't understand much about the magic that governed the bond that Fergus and I had, only that not everyone found their bonded partner.

"They were. I think maybe my Father wished they weren't." He walked over to a shelf, running his fingers along the spines of books until he found the one he wanted and pulled it out.

"But..." That made no sense. "He's punished you for years because she's no longer alive." Surely he did that because he loved and missed his wife.

"The bond is complicated. Father cared for Mother. They were a good team. From what I recall, she balanced out some of his worst traits. But I think he may have been in love with someone else." Fergus' voice went quiet, and I couldn't tell if he wanted to talk about this or preferred to move on.

I tried to hold my tongue, but I couldn't keep my questions to myself. "My mother?"

He shrugged. "I don't know for sure. For as long as I can remember, I've heard rumors about Father loving someone else. After Aoife told us she knew Father when she was younger, I wondered if maybe it was her that people talked about." He held up the book, changing the subject suddenly. "I once heard of a Seelie fae called Everleigh. I think she lives alone somewhere along the border between the two kingdoms."

I let out a breath. "Well, that's good. She shouldn't be too hard to find."

Fergus placed the book he held onto the desk and flipped it open to a map of Faery. The border with Iadrun ran along the bottom of the page, the Crossing marked with a stone gate. Unseelie occupied most of the bottom two thirds of the map, while Seelie took up a small sliver to the west that opened up to cover the entire northern third. Unfortunately, this meant that the border between the two was long, running north from Iadrun before taking a sharp turn east.

I licked my lips. "Or not."

Fergus grinned. "Lucky we have our own private library. Search for atlases or books that have details about the border. Most will include information on Seelie landowners."

I stared at all the shelves, my hand in my hair. This was going to be impossible. "Or we could wait until Father wakes and ask him where to find this Everleigh person."

"We could. But I don't like your chances of getting anything from your father for the next few days. With any luck, if there's a spell on his mind, it will relax with some time away from Unseelie."

I pressed my lips together. "By which time it might be too late for Mother."

Fergus nodded, then his eyes narrowed. "Did you have something better to do than spend time with the prince of your dreams today?"

My eyebrows lifted, and a smile crept across my lips no matter how hard I tried to keep it away. "The what of my what?"

"You heard me." Fergus' eyes danced.

"You're very sure of yourself, Prince Fergus." And this conversation was skirting territory we'd avoided since getting out of our respective prisons.

He placed a hand on his chest, in that way I'd seen him do so often. "I'm a prince. Everyone wants to spend time with me. Or so they tell me."

"Well, this might come as a shock—"

He shook his head, placed his fingers in his ears and closed his eyes. "Not listening. Not listening." He cracked one eye open. "It's a rule, you know. If a prince doesn't want to hear something, he doesn't have to."

I pursed my lips. "Sounds like the prince is making up rules to suit himself."

He grinned, pulled a book from the shelf and tossed it to me. "That is another thing a prince may do because he's, you know, a prince."

I settled down at the desk, still smiling.

He sat across from me, looking over the first book he'd pulled from the shelves. "Crystal isn't my girlfriend," he offered.

My eyes shot up to meet his. "She's not?" I'd been certain there was something between them. They looked so comfortable together.

He shook his head. "Not now, not ever. She is third in command of the Wild Hunt. After me. And Jax."

"There are girls in the Wild Hunt?" Somehow, I'd always imagined they were all males. Probably because of the masks.

"Plenty. Crystal is one of my most fearsome."

"I'll keep that in mind." I dropped my head back to the book to hide the smile that wanted to form on my lips, hoping I didn't look as relieved as I felt that they were nothing more than friends.

I searched through book after book and found nothing. When my backside was numb, I got to my feet and walked a lap of the room, stretching out my back. "So, your mother left you this island without your father knowing it existed?"

Fergus looked up and nodded. "It was a..." He cleared his throat. "A wedding gift. For my future ... wedding."

My mouth fell open. I hadn't expected the Mother who'd died when he was four to leave him a gift for something so far in his future.

"The enchanted letter she left for me contained directions to this place. She said I would need somewhere safe to bring my ... betrothed." His cheeks colored, and he dipped his head. "Somewhere that was neither Seelie nor Unseelie." He took a pen from the jar on the desk and tapped an end against the pages of the book he was looking through as he spoke.

He was talking of our bond. "She approved of us." My words came out as a whisper.

He placed the pen on the desk, his eyes slowly rising to meet mine. "It would seem so. You're surprised?"

I nodded. "Mother said a marriage between the two kingdoms wouldn't be accepted by anyone in either kingdom. I guess I just assumed she literally meant no one. I mean, she wasn't exactly for it." That Fergus' mother thought Fergus and I might need a place together that was away from everything else warmed my heart.

"Long before Mother's time, a relative of hers who was bonded to a Seelie fae lived on this island. They lived here happily for many years. I guess she knew better than to condemn something before giving it a chance."

Did he say that because I wanted to return to Iadrun? "I haven't condemned—"

"Relax, Bria. It wasn't a dig. Not at you, anyway. Whatever you want to do, it's your choice."

He got to his feet and stretched his arms above his head. "I might have found something."

I walked around the desk to stand beside him. His book was open to a map. The Azure River ran across the bottom. Far east of the Border Bridge, just inside the Seelie Kingdom was a small parcel of land marked with the name Everleigh. "You think that's the Everleigh we're looking for?"

He tilted his head. "Seems as good a place as any to start."

My heart jumped. "I didn't think we'd find anything. You're amazing!" We might actually discover what was going on with Father. And Mother. It suddenly felt like everything was moving in the right direction and I couldn't help but smile.

Fergus narrowed his eyes. "So, you're admitting you're glad you spent the time you could have been sleeping sitting in a room with me?"

More glad than he would ever know. I plucked the book from his fingers and walked out the door, checking my smile. "I admit nothing."

SEVEN

I⟨T WAS⟩ mid-morning by the time we exited the library. I hadn't realized so much time had passed while we were in there, but walking through the corridors of Fergus' home, I felt a huge weight lift from me. He took me outside to sit beside the pool in the sun. It was humid and hot, even in the shade. As I made myself comfortable in the cushioned chair, a tall tumbler of iced water—condensation dripping down the outside of the glass—and a bowl of fruit salad appeared on the table in front of me. I glanced Fergus' way.

He shrugged, tucking into the identical bowl of fruit in front of him. "Eat up. You're going to need all the strength you can get if you want to visit Everleigh today."

"Today?" I was wondering how best to broach the subject of visiting Everleigh sooner rather than later, and now I didn't need to. "Don't you have commitments with the Wild Hunt?" And commitments to Unseelie.

"I do." He jabbed his fork into a slice of green melon and put it in his mouth. "But not until later. I want to get Father back, but there's no way I'm risking the Wild Hunt against the queen's forces when they haven't rested long enough to regain their strength. The Wild Hunt rides to Unseelie at dusk." He cast a glance at the sun, high in the sky. "Which still gives us plenty of time to get some answers."

"What answers?" Jax and Willow wandered up the poolside steps from down at the beach. Both were wearing shorts and baggy shirts, and carrying their shoes. Willow had her long blonde hair pulled up into a knot on the top of her head and looked the least like a princess—and the most relaxed—I'd ever seen her.

"Father mentioned a woman he wanted me to find." I shrugged. "Maybe she can tell me where Mother is. Or what's wrong with Father."

Willow picked a slice of yellow fruit from Fergus' bowl with her fingers. He batted her hand away. "You know you can get your own."

She grinned. "Of course. But it's more fun to take yours."

Fergus huffed.

Willow looked at me. "We thought—me and Jax—that we might ride to Holbeck and double check your home. Jax can glamour himself into a long-lost relative of yours and ask around. Double check Aoife isn't there and see how long it's been since she was. We were going to see if you wanted to come, but since it looks like you have other plans, do you mind if we go, anyway?"

I didn't mind. I was humbled that they wanted to do such a thing. Mother was nothing to them but a Seelie enemy, someone they'd both met only one time. "That would be amazing, but only if it doesn't make you too tired to go to Unseelie later." I looked at Jax, assuming Willow wouldn't join the Wild Hunt. I didn't want to be responsible for him not being able to do whatever Fergus expected of him later.

Jax shook his head. "We'll be fine. Riding to Iadrun isn't taxing, and we're taking every member of the Wild Hunt to Unseelie tonight to rescue the king. Until then we have a few hours to fill, and I need to make amends." There was an apology in Jax's eyes.

Fergus lifted an eyebrow. "Amends?"

I shook my head. "It's nothing, Fergus. Don't worry. And thank you, Jax. I'd already forgiven you, and I appreciate your help."

I checked on Father, who was sleeping like the dead, and we were traveling through the sky on Raven and Obsidian a few minutes later with Buttercup running like a puppy at our sides. She kept looking up at Fergus or at me and she loped along beside us, as if we might disappear for months on end again.

We rode above the ocean—Faery coming into view long after Lanwick had disappeared behind us—and flew the horses above the Unseelie side of the Azure River until Fergus decided we were close enough to cross the border and drop down into Seelie territory.

My heart pounded loudly in my ears as the horse's hooves touched the Seelie ground. What Fergus and I were doing was not allowed. Seelie and Unseelie fae were not to cross their borders— some old fae law written years before. Technically, it was only Fergus in the wrong since I was Seelie, but I doubted that would matter much to Rhiannon if she caught us here.

We left the river, making our way up the steep incline of the nearest hill. Birds chirped and behind us, the rushing of the river sounded. As the horses found their footing on even ground at the top of the hill, I slid from Raven's back, staring out across the craggy rocks and peaks that melted into lush shamrock colored forest before flattening to an indigo lake. I couldn't stop staring at the view, my eyes flitting from one piece of scenery to the next. "The colors here are unbelievable. I've never seen sky such a deep shade of..." I didn't even know what shade it was.

"Lapis?" Fergus smiled.

I nodded, my gaze catching on a bird with orange wings. "Yes! Colors aren't so vibrant in Iadrun as they are here in Seelie."

He shook his head. "It's not because you're in Seelie. These lands are part of the Court of Light."

"Because it's always light here?" That sounded more like a curse.

Fergus shook his head again, a smile forming on his lips. "Meaning that the light here—the color—is like nothing you've ever seen before. It's even better at night. The sky isn't black, it's differing shades of deep green, blue and purple."

"It sounds amazing."

Fergus lifted a shoulder like he didn't agree. "Some of the most dangerous fae in Faery hail from the Court of Light, so it's wise to keep your wits about you. Plus, this place is full of dreamers." He spoke the last sentence with scorn, like dreamers were worse than dangerous fae.

"Dreamers?"

"Yes. Artists, sculptors, actors, writers. Pretentious fae who think everyone should love their work just because they've spent time creating it."

The disdain in his voice confused me. "I'm sure they can't all be like that."

"Trust me. They are." His jaw was set.

I frowned. "But ... you're an artist. You make the most amazing..." My voice trailed off. Just because I couldn't see anyone around us, didn't mean I was certain there was no one around. I would not say *music* and risk getting Fergus into trouble. Besides, he knew what I meant. "And you're only pretentious sometimes. And usually not over art."

A smile crept onto his face, though he tried to hide it. "I aim to please." He cast me a sidelong glance, throwing the words I'd used earlier back at me. His smile disappeared. "Can't be an artist when your canvas is illegal."

That was true. But there was an answer. It surprised me no one had suggested it to him before now. "You're going to be king. Once you are, you can pass a new law, then none of the arts would be illegal."

He blew out a breath, shaking his head. "If only it were that easy. The law you speak of, it was decided upon by the monarchy of both kingdoms after an agreement from each kingdom's highest-ranking lords. I see no chance of an arrangement like that between Seelie and Unseelie ever happening again. Especially not over something so trivial."

I shook my head. "I think you could make it happen. If you wanted to." Or he could pass a law that governed only his kingdom, though I understood why he would want to bring music back to the whole of Faery.

He smiled softly. "I appreciate the compliment, but you put far too much weight in my negotiation skills."

"It's not about that, Fergus. It's about how much you want it. And I think, if you listened to your heart, you'd find you want very much to stop hiding the things you love so much." I was no longer only speaking of music, but of the Wild Hunt, too. Once he was king, the Wild Hunt would no longer have to bring humans to Faery for the king the way they did now. Fergus had once told me he thought the Wild Hunt's purpose should be to ease the dying from this life to the next. Without the king controlling them—with Fergus in charge—he could make certain this was their purpose.

"A good king should have the welfare of his kingdom at heart not only his own wants and needs."

"A great king would make both happen. Because I guarantee, if you want it with all your heart, there are many others who feel the same way."

He looked out across the lands stretching below us. "I think, Briony Ridgewing, that your family must once have hailed from the Court of Light."

"Well, it is beautiful here. The colors call to me." Of all the places I'd been in Faery, this felt the most like ... me. Apart from Fergus' island. His island felt like home.

He shook his head. "Not because of that."

"Then why?"

"Because you're as much a dreamer as the artists who live here."

We rode down the ragged hills until we reached the forest that enclosed the parcel of land with Everleigh's name on it. Fergus hesitated at the edge.

"What?" I asked.

"This part of the Light Forest is dangerous. If we're set upon, take to the sky and ride back to Lanwick. Don't wait for me."

His tone was so serious, all I could do was nod and twist my sweating hands around the reins. "Is that a likely occurrence?"

Fergus shook his head. "I don't think so. Most of the fae in this forest travel alone, and they know I'm stronger than them. But if we were to run into a group of them..." He raised his shoulders and I wiped my hands on my riding pants. A group could easily overpower us, especially if they took us by surprise.

He needn't have worried. We found Everleigh's cottage in a small clearing without coming across another fae. Smoke puffed from a chimney above the thatched roof, and a stone pathway welcomed us to the front porch.

We left the horses to graze, and I tapped on the door. I couldn't stand still while I waited for it to swing open. Could this woman help Father? Could she tell me where Mother was, or if she was still alive?

The door opened a crack, but whoever was behind it said nothing.

I cast a nervous glance in Fergus' direction, realizing suddenly how much I wanted this visit to go well. "Everleigh?"

"Don't want any." The woman's voice was old and raspy.

"Oh, we're not selling anything. I just wanted to—"

"Don't want it." The door slammed shut.

I glanced at Fergus again. He lifted his eyebrows and nodded to the door, indicating I should try a second time. I drew in a deep breath, raised the knocker and tapped three times, wondering how many people the woman encountered all the way out here in the woods, selling their wares at her door. This time, when the door opened a slit, I didn't give her the chance to speak. "You know my parents."

There was a beat of silence on the other side of the door. "I don't think so. I've entertained no visitors for many a year. And I do not wish to see any now."

"Not even to save a life?" I glanced again at Fergus, looking for support. He could chime in at any time he liked, offer a suggestion of how we might get inside, use his prince card to get the door open. If he didn't, we may have come all this way for nothing.

"I'm no healer," the voice rasped.

The door creaked again and started to shut. I stuck my boot into the gap to keep it from closing. "I don't need a healer. I need you. My mother's name is Aoife. Ridgewing." A pleading note crept into my voice, so desperate was I that she talk to us.

"It cannot be." The door opened, so slowly I wanted to slap at it with my hand. When it was fully ajar, a petite old woman stepped up to the threshold. "Aoife Ridgewing?" Her gray hair was pulled back into a bun showing off a pair of delicately pointed ears, and she wore spectacles low on her nose. A white apron covered her green dress, and she squinted at me over top of those glasses.

I nodded. "I'm her daughter—"

Everleigh stepped forward, grabbed a handful of my hair near the scalp and placed her other hand on my shoulder to hold me still. Fergus moved beside me, but I shook my head, my hair pulling in the old woman's hand. I didn't need his help. At least, I didn't need it yet.

Burning heat crept onto my face. So many months had passed since anyone had stared at my ears I'd almost forgotten I was different. The fingers in my hair brought my humiliation rushing back. Refusing to give in to it, I lifted my chin and stared at the old woman.

Everleigh pulled the remaining hair away from my ears, then gave a single nod. "Briony Ridgewing. I thought you were dead." She released her grip on my hair.

I rubbed my scalp, unsure if she was happy to see me, or if she wished me to turn around and leave. Her body language gave nothing away. "As did most of Faery, from what I can tell. Mother faked our deaths. I've lived in Iadrun my whole life and only recently discovered I was fae."

She nodded, speaking as if I hadn't said a word. "Yes. I see it now. You look just like her."

Her eyes flicked to Fergus, and she took a staggering step back. "You bring an Unseelie with you? You dare to bring him into our kingdom?" Shaking her head, she retreated farther back into her cottage.

I put up a hand to stop her slamming the door. "He's a friend."

Her eyes narrowed. "The Prince of Unseelie is no friend of this kingdom."

I straightened my shoulders. "Perhaps. But he's a friend of mine and he will not hurt you. My mother is missing, and my father is confused, though he told me to come to you. Prince Fergus is helping with my search. I trust him. You can, too." He was one of the few people in Faery I trusted.

Everleigh's shrewd eyes ran over Fergus before finally nodding. "Very well. Come in. Both of you. But only because I can see you're truly Aoife's daughter."

Once Fergus and I were settled upon her couch—so small, the two of us were almost sitting on top of each other, our body's touching from shoulder to knee—each with a cup of tea in our hands, and she was settled on a rocker in front of the glowing fire, she looked expectantly at me.

Her cottage was tiny and filled to overflowing with furniture. There was only just enough room between the couch Fergus and I sat on and the coffee table in front of it for our knees to fit, yet somehow, Buttercup squeezed in there too, her head lounging across one of Fergus' feet. An easel sat in a sunny corner with an unfinished painting on it, and the walls of the cottage displayed other similar paintings. Everleigh must be one of the artists Fergus disliked so much.

I didn't know what to ask, so I started with the most obvious question. "Why did Father tell me to find you?"

She took a sip of her drink. "I'm not sure. Did you not consider asking him?" Her eyes narrowed. "I believe I heard Myles Ridgewing also died many years ago." She glared at Fergus. "By the hand of the Unseelie King."

I drew in a breath. "I thought so, too. But we found him just yesterday. In Unseelie, working for the king. He's not … himself. I don't know what's wrong with him. He doesn't recognize me, though he seems to recall that Aoife and Bria were important to him."

Everleigh gave a slow nod before glancing again at Fergus. "A spell?"

Fergus leaned forward and put his cup on the table before resting back in the chair. "I believe so."

"An Unseelie spell?" She looked my way, her mouth set in a grim line. She didn't speak the words, but it seemed certain she wanted to say, *see what the Unseelie do to us.*

Fergus nodded. "Myles is no longer in Unseelie. With luck and his strength, the spell may abate."

"You've brought him to Seelie?" Her eyebrows lifted, and she sat forward.

Fergus shook his head and licked his lips. "Not exactly."

I hoped Everleigh didn't push for more information because Fergus wouldn't tell her anything about Lanwick Island.

Everleigh's eyes remained on Fergus and he met her gaze. Finally, she pulled her lips down and nodded. "Good for you," she murmured, settling back on her rocker like she understood exactly where Father was.

When she spoke no further, I said, "So why did he send me here?"

"I don't know, child. I haven't spoken to him in many years. But he came to me in my dreams on the night of All Hallows Eve. As he has done that night same for many a year."

"He told me that you said I could fly and Mother was dead."

She gave a slow nod. "Always the same dream, year after year. A young girl..." She looked me over. "You. High in the sky, then Myles watching while King Aengus killed your mother. It never made any sense to me, especially given I thought you all dead."

It made no sense to me either. "You knew Mother? Before she took me to Iadrun?"

"I've known your mother since she was a babe, and Myles since the two of them married. My home was always a safe place for her, should she need it. For Myles, too. But now I'm old and ill-equipped to keep anyone safe." She took a last gulp of her tea and placed the cup on the side table next to her chair.

"You think he sent me here because I require a safe place?"

Her gaze flicked to Fergus. I put my hand on his knee. "I don't now and never will need to hide from the Prince of the Unseelie Kingdom."

Everleigh's lips turned down again, like she disagreed.

This wasn't getting us anywhere. If Everleigh didn't know why Father had sent me here, then she wasn't the help we'd hoped. But I intended to get some information from her. If she knew Mother as a child, perhaps she'd tell me more about the woman I wondered if I'd ever known. "Can you tell me what my mother was like when you knew her?"

A smile settled on Everleigh's face and her eyes fell somewhere distant. She didn't need any extra prodding to speak of Mother when she was young. "Aoife was the most beautiful child. Inside and out. She had time for everyone, always wanted to help, especially those less fortunate than herself. She was the light of her parent's life and it brought a smile to everyone's faces to see the young family together, they were so happy."

That was lovely. But not helpful. "I don't see—"

Everleigh's smile faltered. "But life is seldom that good for very long, and one day, while out in the forest close to the border with Unseelie, Aoife's mother was set upon and killed. By a group of Unseelie." Everleigh cast Fergus a disparaging glance. "Life changed for your mother after that."

"Wait. Her mother was killed?" Mother had shared no details of her life in Faery. She told me her parents were dead, but not that her mother was murdered.

Everleigh nodded. "Her father, the king, remarried not long after, and they were blessed by a child early in their marriage. But the king was still overcome with grief, and he withdrew from life as it had been, spending much time riding alone to his outer territories, checking on his people, and leaving his beloved daughter with her new mother and sister. He'd go away for months on end, leaving Aoife with a stranger for a mother."

"A stranger that her Father loved enough to marry." Gooseflesh settled on my skin. I had a bad feeling about this story and wanted Everleigh to reassure me.

She let out a sigh. "I suppose he loved her. But never in the way he loved his first wife, and Adriata knew it. With each day her husband spent away from her, she grew angrier. And the only person left to take her anger out on was Aoife. While she doted on her own daughter—"

"Rhiannon?"

Everleigh gave a single nod. "While she doted on Rhiannon, she turned Aoife into a virtual slave. Aoife became the queen's personal cook and housemaid. She wasn't allowed to use her magic to get through her chores, Adriata cast a spell so that if she tried, it would cause Aoife excruciating pain. She moved Aoife from her large rooms on the top floor of the castle to sleep in the basement with the rats. After that, we rarely saw the young princess, even at official events. They fed her on food scraps and she grew so thin that when she went out in public, her old clothing hung loosely off her body."

"Didn't anyone step in? There must have been someone who saw it happening." My voice was pitched high with horror. Poor Mother. No wonder she'd run from Faery. No wonder she'd never wanted to return.

"We all saw it happening, child. But the king was disinterested in anything to do with the castle, and content to let his new queen do as she saw fit. I don't believe the king knew how your mother suffered, otherwise I'm sure he would have helped her. He did love her." She gave me a smile. "As for the rest of us..." She shook her head. "The new queen and her daughter held a privileged position, protected by their home in the castle. No one but the king could stop them doing as they liked, and he'd already proved he had no intention. There was nothing anyone could do but watch as our beautiful princess rotted away in the bowels of that castle."

Fergus plucked my hand from his knee. I'd been gripping him so tightly, I'd probably left a bruise. He slipped his hand into mine and gave it a gentle squeeze.

I blew out a breath, trying to relax. I couldn't help but put myself in Mother's place, to imagine how terrifying it must have been for her to lose her mother, her father, and her home, all within a few short months. I didn't know how she'd survived. "She was imprisoned beneath the castle her entire childhood unless she was doing chores for the queen?" I'd spent time beneath that castle. It was no place for a child. It was no place for anyone.

"Oh, no." Everleigh shook her head. "As she became a teenager, so long as Aoife finished her chores and so long as she was never seen at court, Adriata didn't care what Aoife did with the small amount of spare time she had left in her day. Aoife put that time to good use. If she heard someone was hurt, she hunted them out and tried to heal them with roots and leaves from the forest. If someone was sad, she made them smile. The people still loved her—that didn't change a bit for her time beneath that castle. But every time we saw her, it seemed she grew weaker from lack of food and from lack of love. We feared she might wither away and die."

A lump formed in my throat, especially when I recalled the childhood mother had given me. I'd had laughter and fun, and plenty to eat. I'd had my own problems to deal with, but they never included being locked up or forced to serve someone. "How did she get away from her stepmother? Was it when she met Father?" I shook my head, questions coming too fast for Everleigh to answer. "How did she meet him?"

Everleigh put up a finger. "You move too fast, child. Her life wasn't saved by meeting your father, it was saved by making a friend."

Fergus gave my hand another squeeze.

I blew out a breath. I wanted to hear this entire story, and I wanted it now. "Okay. How did she make a friend?"

With a smile, Everleigh settled back in her chair, pushing with her toes until it rocked ever so slightly. "She went searching for wild blueberries to put in a pie for dinner. Blueberries only grow near the Crossing, so she travelled through the tunnel in search of them."

"There are tunnels in Seelie as well?" Somehow, I'd never imagined there to be.

Fergus shook his head. "Just the one. Between the Seelie Castle and the Crossing."

Everleigh nodded, agreeing. "It's also the only place the border between Seelie and Unseelie is poorly marked. Aoife wandered across the border without realizing in her search for berries and instead found a knife pointed at her heart. Held by an Unseelie girl."

Fergus sat forward. I guessed he hadn't heard this story, either, but something in it piqued his interest.

Everleigh shook her head. "I don't know how your mother managed it, but she talked the girl out of killing her and the two of them talked until dusk. Aoife went back the next day, and the two spent time together again. By the end of the second day, they were firm friends."

"Mother," whispered Fergus.

Everleigh nodded. "Yes." Her eyes grew distant, her voice wistful. "Aoife loved your mother, and I believe Indira loved Aoife, though I never met her."

I thought so, too. But I wasn't following what Everleigh was telling us. "So Indira convinced Mother not to return to Seelie?"

"Indira was the daughter of the lord of the Winter Court. As such, she spent much time at the Unseelie castle. She grew up with Prince Aengus Blackwood, and their friendship was strong. The day she brought Aengus to meet Aoife was the day he..." Everleigh's voice trailed off as she looked at Fergus.

"Fell in love," he finished. He'd guessed that much about his father.

"I believe so," she said, eyes downcast. "Once he realized why Aoife rushed away at the end of every day, he searched out the Seelie King as he visited his people here in the Court of Light. Aengus petitioned for him to allow Aoife to live like a princess once more." She shrugged. "Or to live like a person, I guess, rather than as a rat beneath the castle. The king promised he hadn't known how bad it was for Aoife. He returned home and returned Aoife to her rightful place as princess and next in line for the crown.

"And she kept seeing Indira and Aengus?" I asked.

"She did. Once she met Myles, she took him to meet them, too. For a time, the four were the best of friends. But when two men love one woman, things often turn bad. Your mother chose Myles, much to her own father's disgust, and Aengus couldn't bear it. He pretended to be happy, but he was jealous of Myles. The two argued—over what, I do not know—but it caused a rift between them all." She closed her eyes. "So many things changed in Faery because of that friendship."

"What things?"

She lifted a shoulder. "While Aoife lived in the basement, Rhiannon was sure she would be queen. When the king restored Aoife to the castle, he made it clear his firstborn would rule and Rhiannon lost that hope. She grew angry and hateful."

Fergus stiffened at the sound of Rhiannon's name. I squeezed his hand. She'd hurt him badly, and more than once, it was no wonder he didn't like to hear about her.

"Aengus changed after that, too. He became angrier. Meaner." Everleigh shrugged. "He wasn't like that when Aoife knew him. Maybe he wouldn't be the way he is now had he never met her—he certainly wouldn't have had his heart broken by her. But I can't wish for that because I will always be certain Aoife survived those awful years because of the time she spent with Indira and then Aengus."

I sighed. Mother's best friends had come from the rival kingdom. Her judgment told her they were good people. Yet that same judgment had made her keep Fergus and I apart. I didn't even know why I was upset about that. I didn't want Fergus the way the magic wanted me to. I guess it just hurt that Mother and the king had decided we weren't good enough for each other, when the two of them had seen past their own differences when they needed to.

"What's wrong, child?"

I shook my head. I wasn't sharing those thoughts. "I guess I just hoped for ... something more." A tidbit that might help me find Mother. Or something that would tell us what was wrong with Father. Anything, really, other than what she'd told us.

Everleigh leaned her head back against her chair and surveyed me. "You mean Rhiannon."

I shrugged. I doubted more childhood stories would help. I honestly didn't know what I wanted from her.

Everleigh either didn't notice my reluctance or didn't care. "She's ambitious, that one." Her lips pursed.

Fine, if we were talking about her, there was one question I really wanted answered. "Do you think Mother could be working with her?" It seemed as if Everleigh knew Mother and Rhiannon better than anyone else I had met in Faery. I wanted her to put my mind at ease.

Everleigh considered a moment. "It's possible. But unlikely, I think. I don't believe the two ever particularly liked each other. I'd suggest it far more likely Rhiannon befriended your mother just to get to Aoife's intensifier. She must be careful."

I glanced at Fergus, hoping he might translate. I had no idea what that meant.

He twisted in our small seat to face me, our knees bumping. "In Seelie, when a crown prince or princess is born, they are given an heirloom. The moment he or she takes their crown, the heirloom draws in excess and unused magic from around the realm and passes it on to the new monarch, ensuring they have more magic than anyone else in the kingdom. The heirloom is a unique item for each prince or princess."

"Is that what the royal sword is? An intensifier?"

Fergus paled. He shook his head, but his words were unsure. "No. I mean, maybe, but I've never heard them referred to as the same thing." He glanced at Everleigh. "But if Rhiannon gets hold of the royal sword *and* Aoife's intensifier, she'll be more powerful than anyone has ever been in Faery."

I swallowed. "And Rhiannon will have an intensifier of her own. Right?"

Fergus shook his head. "I don't think she does. She was never meant to become queen. And since the real queen is still alive, her intensifier unused, there was no need for Rhiannon to have one. Plus, she's one of the strongest in the realm in her own right. I wouldn't expect her to need one."

Clearly, Rhiannon wasn't of the same opinion on that matter. Suddenly, her hunt for power made more sense. "Can she use Mother's? Because she holds the crown?"

Everleigh lifted her shoulders. "These are unusual times..."

I waited for her to finish, but she seemed uninclined to say more. "So, she can use it?"

Everleigh's lips pressed together. "Technically, no, she shouldn't be able to. But there has never in the past been a time where there were two fully working and unused intensifiers within the realm, yet no intensifier on the throne..." Her voice trailed off again and she pressed her wrinkled fingers to her lips. "Rhiannon was always good at spells. I don't believe she's currently any more powerful than she ever was, but perhaps she knows a spell that will take the power from someone else's intensifier and give it to herself." She shrugged. "I'd guess she's searching for your intensifier and has dragged Aoife in to help."

"Or perhaps Aoife is just pretending to help her," added Fergus. "Leading her away from the intensifier, rather than toward it."

I appreciated Fergus seeing the best in Mother though I wasn't sure it was founded, but I heard something else in Everleigh's words. "I don't have an intensifier." I shook my head. "I don't. The only heirloom we ever owned was..." I licked my lips as I looked at Fergus. "That ugly vase Mother smashed over Xion's head when he came to our home." The night Fergus injured Mother.

Everleigh shook her head. "If your Mother broke it, I can guarantee it wasn't an intensifier."

"We had nothing else. Perhaps she left it in Faery when she took me to Iadrun." She'd never planned for either of us to become queen, let alone return to Faery. We didn't need intensifiers.

Everleigh's eyes brightened, her thoughts heading in another direction. "I heard the queen captured a young woman and held her beneath the castle awaiting execution as an imposter. Is that true?"

I blinked at the speedy change of topic. "I believe you're referring to me. She captured me and held me in her prison, but I'm no imposter. Aoife Ridgewing is my mother."

Everleigh nodded, her eyes thoughtful. "Didn't you ever wonder why Rhiannon held you there for so long without killing you?"

My mouth fell open as I searched for an answer to her question. I hadn't wondered. Not really. Fergus had suggested she was preparing for my execution, but thinking on that now, I doubted she would allow me to languish for so many weeks without it happening.

"No?" Everleigh asked.

Her question suddenly made sense. "You think my intensifier is why she didn't kill me outright?"

Fergus nodded, his tone musing. "She was breaking you down, so when the time came, you would be so hurt and hungry that you would hand over anything to get out of there. Including your intensifier."

I shook my head. "She never meant to let me out. She wanted me to tell her where to find my intensifier, then she was going to kill me." I wasn't surprised, but knowing how close I'd come to dying in there made me sick. Even if I'd wanted to, I could never have told her what she wanted to know because I didn't know where that intensifier was myself.

Fergus elbowed me. "Lucky your magic made an appearance."

"Lucky I was annoyed enough at her to use it."

We left Everleigh's home soon after, our mood somber as we rode through the forest. I had survived death at my aunt's hands because she wanted some magical relic I knew nothing of. "I need to go to my cottage in Iadrun. To search for this intensifier thing."

Fergus nodded, his face grim. He looked up at the grey sky through the canopy of trees. It was around midday. "We have time now."

Now sounded perfect, though the chance of finding anything was slim. If Mother really had hidden some artifact at my home, Rhiannon would have surely found it. And if she had Mother on her side—either willingly or forcefully—then it was only a matter of time before Mother gave up the details of her own intensifier. If she hadn't done so by now.

A ball of fear formed in my chest. Rhiannon's recent movement into Unseelie indicated she felt like no one could stop her.

Perhaps no one could.

Maybe we were too late, and she was already the most powerful fae in Faery.

I was so lost in my thoughts I didn't notice the way Raven's ears flattened against her head until her pace increased. I turned to look over my shoulder for whatever had spooked her—Fergus had warned me to stay vigilant while in the Light Forest. I'd been too busy thinking about what Everleigh told us to watch the surrounding forest. Fergus must have been just as distracted because he hadn't noticed the horses tension either.

As I turned, something solid hit me in the back of the head. The blow was so hard, it tipped me from my place on Raven's back and I slid toward the ground. I threw my hand out to brace my fall and as I hit, white hot pain bloomed in my wrist.

It shot up to my shoulder. Fergus yelled, and blackness stole my vision.

EIGHT

I CAME TO lying on my back on the musty forest floor to the sound of Fergus groaning. I turned my head to find him also on the ground a little way from me. Standing over him were three fae, the likes of which I'd never seen before. They were tall and broad, their biceps bigger than my head. From the neck down, they could have been human. From the neck up they were reptilian, their snake-like faces covered in green scales and with a forked tongue that flicked in and out of their mouths. One crouched beside Fergus and pried his lips apart while another filled his mouth with white powder. Fergus kicked and bucked but didn't seem able to stop them.

I pushed to my feet. My wrist cried out in pain and the lump on my head made the world spin. "Leave him alone." My voice was rough. I called on my magic. Even if it didn't do as I expected—which seemed likely—it might at least frighten them into stopping whatever they were doing. Before I could use it, a fourth creature approached me from behind, dug his fingers into my shoulders and forced me back to the ground.

"Be still," he hissed, his face beside my head. "Or you're for the same treatment as your friend."

The three other fae stepped back from Fergus and stood watching while he rolled onto his stomach, braced himself on his elbows and spat the white substance onto the ground. One of them hissed words I couldn't hear, a taunt to which Fergus reacted by spitting at the fae's feet. The fae drew his foot back and kicked the Unseelie Prince in the side, so hard I was certain I heard something crack. A muffled cry sprang from my lips. Fergus curled around himself, making a ball on the forest floor.

No. This was not happening. They may have massive muscles, but I was quick, and I knew a thing or two about fighting. I rolled down to my back, drew my knees up to my chest, then kicked backward over my head, connecting with the scaled face of my attacker. It was an excellent shot and would have knocked any human in that same position out cold, or at least rendered them unable to move for a few minutes from the pain. But my fae attacker didn't even blink. He pushed my legs down, coming around to the side of my body and holding me against the ground with his arm. He called to his friends with a voice that slithered down my spine. "Bring me the salt."

As I struggled—barely moving beneath the bulk of my attacker—one of the three with Fergus wandered over to us.

Whatever they'd done to Fergus looked bad. The white powder they'd poured into his mouth was mostly red when he spat it out, and I could only assume he was spitting blood. If he could get up and fight back, he would have, but since no one was holding him down, I had to assume the white powder stole his energy. Or his magic.

I couldn't let them do the same to me. "Let us go! We don't want to fight you."

The fae wandering over to me pulled his wide mouth back into a smile. "That is good," he hissed. "Because it would appear˙ you are overpowered." He nodded to the one holding me down, who slipped his dirty finger between my lips and pried my mouth open. I tried to bite him, but he'd done this before, and his finger came nowhere near my teeth.

The powder was salt—like he'd said—and the first grains stung the back of my throat and made me gag. He filled my mouth to overflowing before I could blink. For a moment, it just tasted revolting. Then it felt like someone was scraping my insides out with a hundred blunt knives. All my energy flowed from my body and it was all I could do to keep my head from rocking forward onto my chest.

The fae released his grip on me and I rolled to my stomach, spitting it from my mouth. The salt was globby and streaked with blood.

"Bria ... spit it ... all out!" Speaking sounded like an effort as Fergus panted between words. "If you swallow the grains ... they will burn you from the inside out."

I was already doing as he suggested. I'd never tasted anything so bad. Or felt anything so painful. Tears streamed from my eyes. For each mouthful I expelled, there seemed to be another ten still inside my mouth. I rested my head on the cool ground as I purged the substance again and again.

When I was done—which felt like days later but was probably only minutes—I lay still, catching my breath and calling for my magic. I didn't care how faulty it was, or how many shots it took to hit one of them, I would kill these bastards for attacking us.

But my magic wouldn't form.

I lay on my side, watching helplessly as all four fae stood over Fergus.

"Where is your sword?" the one with the salt hissed.

Fergus groaned but otherwise voiced no reply.

Salty hissed and kicked Fergus in the back. Fergus' body spasmed, and a scream of pain tore from his lips. "Search him," said Salty.

The other three bent over Fergus, pulling back his cloak and patting down his legs and arms. As they worked, Fergus' magic pooled around him— it was so pale it was almost impossible to see, but it was there. And it gave me hope. If he could do it, I could, too.

The longer the salt was out of my mouth, the more my strength returned. I called up my magic, drawing it around me. It came slowly, forming like a cloak around my body, almost colorless. As I waited, the color deepened, my magic strengthening. With slow movements so as not to draw attention, I pushed myself to sitting.

The fae stopped searching Fergus' body and looked up at Salty. "He doesn't have it."

Fergus lay on his back, panting and with his eyes closed. Globs of blood-covered salt dribbled out the side of his mouth, but his magic was growing in color by the second. He should be back to full strength in a minute or two. With any luck, the panting and lying still were just a cover.

"Kill him," hissed Salty.

"But ... we're meant to take them in," one of the other fae said.

Salty shook his head. "He doesn't know what we're talking about. He's no help to us. Kill him."

The muscles on the arms of the three other fae bulged. There was no magic around them, so it appeared they were going to do this the human way. With their fists.

Fergus' magic wasn't quite back to normal yet, though it would be soon. I searched the forest for Raven, and found her hidden among the trees, her eyes trained on me. All we needed was to get to the horses, then we were safe—they'd fly us away from here.

I focused on the fae who'd held me down, telling my magic it was him I wanted to hit, and with a final plea, I let it go.

The ball of pink shot straight from my hand, hurtling toward my tormenter, and burrowed into his spine. As he toppled forward, Fergus burst to his feet, three balls of magic of the deepest blue I'd ever seen shooting from his hands. The first two balls carved into an eye and a neck of the two remaining fae, each of them dead before they hit the ground. The final ball of magic was for Salty.

It struck him in the stomach, so hard it propelled him backward and into the oak behind him, but not hard enough to kill him outright. He hit with a thud. A band of blue magic wound around his neck, dragging him upward until only the tips of his toes touched the ground. He raked at his neck with his fingers, trying to pull the magic off, but it refused to yield.

"Who sent you?" Fergus snarled, prowling toward the fae. His shoulders were relaxed, his strides loose, but his gait was lethal. I'd never seen him this way, as Prince of the Unseelie Kingdom, standing up for his throne. He was terrifying.

Salty must have thought so, too. He whimpered, pulling harder on the band of magic at his throat, and kicking his legs in an effort to free himself.

"Who. Sent. You?" Fergus stopped in front of the fae, wiping the salt remnants from his chin with the arm of his sleeve.

"R-Rhiannon."

No surprises there.

Fergus nodded. "For what does she require my weapons?"

Salty shook his head so fast the magic cut into his skin and a line of blood dribbled down his scales toward his human-like shoulders.

"Don't know. She doesn't share that information with us."

Fergus gave a slow blink. "And where is she now?"

"How should I know?"

Fergus turned his wrist—the smallest of movements—and the band of magic tightened, pulling Salty back against the tree. The fae gasped for air, but Fergus just folded his arms, waiting.

Salty struggled, kicking his legs and wrestling for breath. "Unseelie. She's in Unseelie. At the castle."

"You were to return to her, after you finished with me?"

Salty nodded. "Please, if you let me go, I'll tell her you don't have it. That you never had it. I'll tell her whatever you want me to tell her."

Fergus gave a slow nod and Salty stopped struggling, perhaps sensing a reprieve. "The same way you were going to let me go a few moments ago?"

Salty began to struggle again, his movements frenzied. "I never would have gone through with it." His fingers dug into his neck, opening up more cuts as he tried to loosen the magic. "You have to believe me."

Fergus smiled at him before turning his hand palm up. A ball of deep blue magic appeared, the color, if possible, even deeper than when he'd used his magic before. "I think I too might like to follow orders."

Salty stared at the ball of magic, shaking his head. "No. Please." His voice shook.

"King Aengus Blackwood—perhaps you've heard of him?" Fergus raised an eyebrow at Salty.

Salty's tongue flicked out and back into his mouth and his body shook as he attempted to break free.

"No? He is the king of the Unseelie fae. And his orders, should anyone attempt to kill the Crown Prince, are to hunt that fae down and give them a long, slow death."

Salty clawed at the magic around his neck. "You don't understand..."

"Oh, I understand completely." Fergus let his magic go, watching as it hit Salty beneath his chin and made a path straight up and into his brain.

Salty was dead before he registered the magic moving. Fergus released the band holding him against the tree and the fae dropped to a pile on the ground.

Fergus turned to me. "Are you all right?"

I let out my breath and nodded, unsure if I trusted myself to speak. I was pretty sure we'd just come extra close to dying, which was looking like a dangerous habit when I was around Fergus. "Are you?"

"Perfect. Now they're dead." He walked over to me and took my injured wrist in his hands. His jaw was set as he passed his magic over me and healed the broken bone. "I'm sorry."

"For what?" It was hardly his fault I'd broken my wrist in a fall.

"Those thugs were after me. You just happened to be in the way."

"Unlike the times people have been after me recently and you've been the unintended casualty?" The pain in my arm disappeared the moment Fergus' magic touched me. I sighed in relief.

Some tension left his face. "Point taken." He held my wrist until he was sure he'd healed it completely.

"What did they want?" I hadn't heard the entire conversation between them all, only something about a weapon.

"My sword." He shook his head. "I never carry one on my body here in Faery—I keep it in the void." He glanced at me to see if I understood. "It's a magical holding cell where I can store items I don't want to carry." There was no need for a sword on your body when you could shoot out magic that killed two fae at once.

"But you carry one in Iadrun." He didn't need to answer. I'd seen it myself when he was with the Wild Hunt. And he had used one in the Unseelie castle when we fought the queen. "Maybe they thought your sword was the Royal Sword."

"Perhaps." Fergus surveyed the bodies lying around us. "Though I don't have any idea why they'd think such a thing. It's nothing special."

I stared at the bloodied salt in the dirt where I'd fallen, more questions coming to my lips. "So, now I'm fae I can't eat salt?" It had never been a problem in Iadrun, but then, neither had a lot of things. "I thought you said salt wasn't harmful." After all, he lived on an island in the middle of the ocean, surrounded by salty water.

Buttercup crept out from behind a log. Fergus bent to pat her. "It isn't. *That* was enchanted salt. The Naga use it as a poison to stun their prey before they beat them to a pulp. I'd say we were about a minute from dead."

"Until you took them down with three blasts of magic at once. That was impressive."

Fergus smiled. "Almost as impressive as you actually hitting one of them. I'm assuming you aimed for that tree over there?" He pointed in the opposite direction to where my magic had gone, light dancing in his eyes.

I punched him in the arm. I'd aimed at the naga. "I'm serious. Three balls of magic at one time is amazing. I can't even deal with one."

Fergus smiled. "You dealt just fine with one." He whistled. The horses trotted out of their hiding places and he checked them over to make sure they weren't hurt. When he spoke again, his head was still down, as he ran his hands over Obsidian. "I was thinking about what you said."

I pulled myself onto Raven, patting her neck once I was comfortable—it surprised me that I found myself more relaxed on the back of this horse than almost any other place I'd ever been. "About what?"

"About how I should think about being king from a viewpoint other than my own."

That wasn't exactly what I'd said, but the sentiment was in there somewhere. "And...?"

Fergus climbed onto Obsidian and directed him into the air, pushing between the tops of the forest trees while Raven and I followed. Neither of us had any wish to come face to face with more naga, and we no longer needed to stay hidden in Seelie. The air was the safest place for the rest of this trip.

"And..." Fergus dropped his chin to his chest, intentionally mumbling. "You might be right."

I grinned. That was an admission I wouldn't hear every day, or perhaps ever again. "I might be what now?"

He pressed his lips together, trying to look stern. It only made him seem like he was trying very hard not to smile. He sighed. "You were right."

"Of course I was." There was no way I was checking my smile. "About what?"

"I stopped hiding what I have." The wind rushed through his hair, whipping the black strands around his face as we crossed over the Azure River and into Unseelie.

"Good for you." Though, I had no idea what that meant.

Fergus licked his lips. He seemed nervous. "What you saw today was the most magic I've ever used at one time. But it's not all the magic I have." At some point, Buttercup had climbed up onto Obsidian in front of Fergus, and she lay stretched out on some invisible magic seat like she was queen of the realm. Unseelie stretched out in front of us, and the border wall sparkled in the distance.

That would explain the deep color of his magic today. I'd never seen it like that. "You hide your power?" I didn't even know that was possible.

He shrugged. "I've spent my entire life doing everything I could not to become king. Being powerless seemed the most likely way to get the result I desired. If I was weak, no one would want me to succeed to the throne because it would leave Unseelie vulnerable to attacks from across the border." He glanced my way. "But I heard what you said earlier, and it made sense. I thought I'd try it, see what I could do. Turns out, I can kill a couple of fae and capture another."

"All without breaking a sweat." I grinned. It had been impressive to watch him kill those naga.

"It was so freeing!" He laughed, then his eyes rounded as he looked at me. "Not the killing. I never like that. But releasing the power."

"You've never told anyone you were hiding it? Shown anyone what you can do? Jax? Willow?"

He shook his head. "I couldn't tell them because that meant admitting what I was doing, which also meant facing the fact that taking the throne was in my future. I've never admitted that to myself."

"You still don't need to. If you don't want to."

He glanced my way, a frown forming between his eyes. "I don't?"

I shook my head. "I won't tell anyone. If you want to keep all that power hidden, that's your choice."

He nodded. "Thank you." We rode for a few more moments before he added, "It was pretty hot though, right? Me saving you from three naga at once?" His eyes twinkled.

I shook my head, trying not to smile. Or agree with him, which I really wanted to do. I shrugged. "It was nothing more than I'd expect from any prince I was travelling with."

"Someone's been here." Fergus stood on the threshold of my cottage on the outskirts of Holbeck.

"You think?" My voice dripped with sarcasm. I was half a step in front of him, the back door ajar in my hand. If I'd thought Xion had destroyed our cottage with his furniture tornado, I'd been wrong. Currently, there was not a space on the floor that didn't have something lying upon it. Our dining chairs were scattered around the room, the stuffing pulled from the seats. Pictures, clothing, cutlery and crockery were all flung over the floor. They'd even scooped the ash from the fireplace and tossed it across the room.

"I wonder if they found what they were searching for?" Fergus mused, as we tip-toed our way into the house.

"I don't think so." Our cottage was small, and from the center of the living area—which was also the kitchen and dining area—I could see into the other three rooms of the house. Mother's bedroom had been given the same treatment. Her mattress was half off her bed, the bedding on the floor. There wasn't a space in her consulting room that didn't have smashed glass laying on it, and herbs were scattered all around the small room. In my bedroom, the bed had been slashed apart.

I swallowed back my tears, my vision distorting as they pooled in my eyes. This house contained my life. Or it had until six months ago when Xion Starguard came crashing into this very room. Now nothing was salvageable. "If they found what they were looking for, they would have stopped tearing the place apart." And they hadn't done that. My guess was that they were looking for the same thing we'd come in search of—my intensifier. If such a thing even existed.

Fergus took another step, toeing away a book so he could put his foot down. Then he bent and began picking up things—or parts of things—around him.

"What are you doing?" I was still staring at the mess in our cottage, my mind stuck on the destruction.

"Tidying up."

His eyes were on me, but I couldn't return his gaze. Everywhere I looked, something I loved lay broken on the ground. A picture with a twisted frame, Mother's favorite mug, the mirror that once hung on the wall of my room. Every piece of my childhood—of my entire life—broken apart.

I didn't recall him moving, but Fergus was suddenly standing in front of me, blocking my view of the messy house. "I'm quite good at tidying."

His words were like a gentle slap to the face and I managed a small smile. "I very much doubt that. *Prince* Fergus."

He clutched his chest, dramatically pretending I'd wounded him. "That hurts. You think because I grew up in a castle, I had other people do my chores?"

My smile grew an increment in width and feeling. I didn't miss the fact that his comment pushed away some of the hopelessness stalking me, and I was grateful. "Oh, I know you did."

He glanced at his feet, scratching the back of his head. "Okay. You might be right." Looking up, he added, "But I come with plenty of other benefits."

As much as he'd made me feel better, I didn't have the energy for this light-hearted banter at the moment. Someone had broken into my home, which was horrifying. Despite my confidence that they'd found nothing, I wasn't certain. And I never would be because I didn't know what exactly they had come in search of. Which also meant I didn't know what we were looking for.

"I'm sure you do." I took a step away, but Fergus caught my wrist.

His fingers on my skin made my breath catch.

The lightest shimmer of blue surrounded him, then he blinked. And everything inside my house righted itself. From one breath to the next, stuffing returned to chairs, crockery became whole, and the ashes made their way back into the hearth. "What good is it bringing a prince to your home if he can't provide a little magic to help out?"

"Thank you." My words weren't enough. It would have taken days to right the contents of the house without his help. Seeing everything back in order eased the worry in my stomach that we were too late, that Rhiannon had already won a war we had only just realized we were fighting.

Fergus frowned, his fingers still around my wrist. "What, no smart response? No insinuation that you can do it better?" He dropped my wrist and held the back of his hand to my forehead. "You must be truly ill."

I stepped out of his grasp, unable to play his game. "This isn't a joke, Fergus. This is my home. People have been here searching for something that could change the way we live our lives. If they found it, I feel like I'm obligated to stop Rhiannon.

HAYLEY OSBORN

And I don't know how." I shook my head. "I'm so out of my depth."

Fergus took my hands, the sparkle gone from his eyes and his face solemn. "Welcome to my world."

"Thanks. But I've been part of it for a while now." The sentence came out harsher than I intended.

Fergus shook his head, ignoring the bite of my words. "Never think I don't get it, Bria. I've spent my entire life feeling like I can't do what's expected of me. The crushing weight that tells me I might not be enough, it's always there, waiting to overwhelm me and convince me I'm right. If we want to beat this, beat her, we can't listen to those voices in our heads. We are enough. We can do this." He swallowed, his voice dropping to a whisper. "We have to."

I nodded. He was right. If we didn't keep trying, Rhiannon would rule over us all, and that would mean an early death for Fergus and me, or at the very least, life lived in a cold dark cell.

"You know…" He dropped my hands and strolled over to the kitchen, opening cupboard doors, peering inside then shutting them again. "A wise woman once convinced me I could make a good king."

I sucked in a deep breath and pulled back my shoulders. Now was not the time to feel sorry for myself. I didn't know if there ever would be a time for that again. None of this was Fergus' fault. He could have walked away at the first sign of trouble. Seelie problems were no problem of his. I was grateful he hadn't. "It's true." I nodded. "That woman *is* very wise."

Fergus turned, surprise twinkling in his eyes at my sudden change of attitude. His gaze made my heart skip. "The wisest," he agreed, opening and shutting another cupboard. "Perhaps she should reconsider her future options. And I don't mean the options she has in Unseelie." The option of a life with him. Even though I didn't want what the bond had thrust upon us, it was a knife through my chest to have him remind me he didn't want it either.

I plastered a smile on my face, hoping he didn't notice. "What other options are there to consider?" As far as I could see, healing in Iadrun was what my future held.

He poked his head around an open cupboard door. "Rumor has it you're a direct descendant from the Seelie Queen. The *real* Seelie Queen."

Oh. That option. I shook my head. "No. That won't ever happen. And even if I wanted it, and even if Mother stood aside, the Seelie people are hardly going to want a queen who hasn't even lived in Faery for an entire cycle of the sun."

Fergus' chin lifted. "Sounds to me like someone has already spent much time considering this."

I hadn't. Not at all. It just seemed logical that no one would want a stranger to rule. "There's nothing to consider."

He carefully closed the cupboard door and stalked over to me. "The lady is very good at handing out advice, not so good at receiving it. Perhaps she wouldn't make the best queen, after all."

I raised my chin, taking the bait. Lacking in energy or not, I enjoyed sparring with him this way. It made everything else we were dealing with seem less important. For a few minutes, anyway. "Oh, I'd make an amazing queen. I just don't want to do it."

He lifted his eyebrows and turned back to the cupboards. "Uh-huh."

"Are you hungry or something? Because I doubt you'll find any food in the house. It's been months since anyone was here."

He shook his head. "I'm searching for your intensifier. Isn't that why we're here?"

It was, but I'd figured that ship had long since sailed. If there was an intensifier in the house, it had left with the people that made the mess of our belongings or it was never here in the first place. "Should I be concerned that the first place you look for such an item of mine is with the food?"

A smile grew on his face. "You should not. The kitchen was not my first choice of potential hiding places."

"Oh, really?" I turned on the spot, wondering where I should start my search. If Mother had hidden something here, she wouldn't have left it any place obvious. I got down on my knees and opened the hatch beneath the cottage, sticking my head through. The roughly dug dirt hole was just big enough to fit three adults. There was nowhere to hide anything and nothing laying upon the dirt. I pulled my head back into the room. "And where would you have looked?"

He strolled toward me, stopping when he was closer than he needed to be. He leaned forward, his breath warm on my cheeks. "Why, your bedroom, of course."

His words sent a delicious shiver along my spine. I met his eyes. "That's very presumptive of you."

He shuffled closer. "How so?" His voice softened and his eyes moved to my lips. He was as close as he could be without actually touching me.

Stars. There was not enough air in this room. And how long had his lips looked like a miniature bow? A very full, very kissable miniature bow. I shook my head. Conversation. We were in the middle of a conversation. I had no need to stare at Fergus Blackwood's lips. "It's presumptive to think I would invite you into my bedroom."

His smile grew wicked. "Oh, I wasn't going to wait to be invited."

There should have been a million rejections to that, but not one came to mind. It was all I could do not to lean into him.

"I also didn't intend to search for anything once I got in there."

A vision of him stretched out on my bed, hands behind his head as he stared at me, made its way into my mind. Stars, what an image. I closed my eyes, trying to pull myself together before smiling up at him. "Tired, are you Prince Fergus? I'm sure I can find you a nice cozy blanket to snuggle up with." I turned away because if I didn't, this was going to go somewhere I had to keep reminding myself that I didn't want.

He reached out and gripped my wrist, pulling me back to him, the distance between us less than it had been before, our arms locked between our chests.

I didn't dare move, because this time, I wasn't sure I could move away. I didn't think I could keep denying our bond.

"Oh, I wasn't planning on sleeping. And I'm sure you'd keep me warmer than any blanket could."

He leaned in. He was going to kiss me. If I wanted to stop him, now was the time.

But I neither wanted to nor did it. Instead, I stretched up on my tiptoes, leaning closer to him, wanting to feel the way I had all those months ago at his naming ceremony when I'd kissed him in front of hundreds of people and hadn't cared. When, in that moment, I hadn't ever wanted to stop kissing him.

He bent closer, brown eyes on me. I drew in a breath and closed my eyes.

And suddenly, he was gone.

He dropped my wrist and stepped away. I slowly opened my eyes. He stood across the room looking out our dirty front window and across our yard at the pocked street, his shoulders heaving.

My cheeks flamed. I was so stupid. Kissing Fergus was always a dumb idea, but by getting so close then walking away, he'd made certain I knew how dumb it was. The magic of our bond was controlling me. I had to keep reminding myself of that.

It took a moment of shocked silence before I could make myself turn away and head for my bedroom. That was the most likely place Mother would have hidden something that belonged to me. Plus, it had a door that I could slam in Fergus Blackwood's face.

"We can't do that." Fergus' voiced drifted to me from across the small room.

I shrugged, not that he would see it; he couldn't even look at me. "Fine with me." It was the stupid bond's fault anyway, nothing else.

Fergus turned before I could reach my room. He looked wretched. "You don't understand."

I shook my head and turned my lips down, hoping to look like I didn't care. I would not beg for answers. If there was more to tell about our bond, he'd had plenty of time to do so. "There's nothing to understand."

He took an uncertain step toward me.

I lifted my chin. He might be used to women begging for his company, but he wouldn't receive that from me.

My movement caused his face to harden until he was sporting a glare of the sort he hadn't directed at me since we first met. "I guess there isn't."

His words hit where he aimed, straight at my heart. Not that I let him see it. I pulled my face into a smile, opening my mouth to agree.

Before I could say anything, the back door smashed open.

In a blink, Fergus moved into the center of the room, standing in a crouch between me and the door, while I stood stock still, recovering from the fright the sound had given me. A sword appeared in Fergus' hand, pulled from the void he kept it in. He was already swinging it in a downward arc when his attacker held up a hand. "Stop! Ferg, it's me. It's Jax."

Fergus pulled his swing. "What in the stars are you still doing here?"

We'd seen no sign of their horses when we arrived and given the time we'd spent in Seelie before coming here, hadn't expected them to still be here.

"Searching for Aoife." Jax looked at me. "Things don't seem quite right here in Holbeck."

"What are you two doing here?" Willow stepped up to the threshold and leaned on the frame of the back door.

"Long story." Fergus released his sword, and it disappeared back into the hole of magic he'd pulled it from. "Did you two make a mess of the house?"

I hoped so. Apart from it being totally disre-spectful to treat someone else's belongings that way, I preferred it was done by people I knew and could question about their motives.

Willow shook her head. "It was like that already. Do you know who did it?"

I shook my head. "Rhiannon? Her thugs?" The thought of those naga going through my things made my skin crawl.

"Are you almost done here?" asked Jax. "We were about to leave."

It was early afternoon. We had plenty of time to reach Lanwick before dusk, and I was almost certain this was a dead end. "Five more minutes?" That would give us enough time to check over the bedrooms for signs of an intensifier.

But instead of heading back into my room, a picture on the front wall caught my eye, and I strolled over to look at it. It was the only one we had of Mother, Father and I together.

I lifted the frame from the wall. Just in case I never saw Mother again, and because I didn't know when I'd get back here, I removed the picture from the frame. Folding it in half, I slipped it into my pocket.

As I did, the window in front of me shattered and something huge barreled through it, landing on top of me.

NINE

I HIT THE ground on my back, my head smashing into the wooden floor so hard my vision wavered. A heavy weight settled on my chest, and fingers crept into my pocket, withdrawing the folded picture. I blinked, trying to clear my sight, but with the picture in hand, my attacker was upright and gone, matted auburn hair swinging as she jumped through the window.

Willow jumped out straight after, followed by Jax. Fergus held out a hand and helped me to my feet. "Are you all right?"

I nodded. It seemed like he asked me that a lot lately. But I wasn't hurt, although I imagined I'd have a bump on the back of my head. "What ... just happened?"

"I'm not sure I know. Someone burst through the window, stole your picture and left."

I knew that much. I moved to look out the broken window. All three of them were gone, but Jax's raised voice reached my ears coming from the backyard, followed by a high-pitched scream. Turning on my heel, I sprinted for the back door.

"Bria! Wait!"

I raced down the steps. Fergus could yell all he wanted, but I wasn't stopping. I recognized that scream. "Selina!" I ran across our shared back yard. And stopped dead. Selina was here all right, but she'd never looked worse. Her beautiful auburn hair was so matted I couldn't imagine her ever getting a comb through it again. Her dress was ripped and dirty. Grime covered her bare feet, making them black, and her arms—and probably feet—had bleeding cuts from where she'd burst through the window.

Willow stood on one side of her, Jax on the other, talking softly. Selina held a knife out in front of her, alternately waving it at Jax and then Willow. "Get back," she snarled. "I'll kill you. I'm not afraid."

"Selina," I called again, drifting toward her. There was no question Jax and Willow could remove that knife from her grip, but I wanted to make sure they did so without hurting her.

Selina looked my way before returning her glare to Willow and Jax. She looked straight through me. For all I knew, she hadn't recognized me.

I moved another step closer. I knew she was scared. Her dealings with the fae until now had been terrifying. Once she realized no one in this yard would hurt her, she'd put the knife down.

I kept my hands out in front of me so she could see them. "Selina. It's me. It's Bria. You can put the knife down. No one wants to—"

Selina launched at me, arms flailing. She wrapped them around my waist and tackled me to the ground, shoving her knife into my arm.

I bit down on a groan as she pulled the knife out, blood dripping from the blade. "Selina! It's me. You have to stop this." The knife arced down toward my face. I threw my head to one side, and it struck the ground. "Selina. Stop!"

"She can't." Willow dive tackled her off me, pushing her onto her back and straddling her waist to pin her against the ground.

I jumped to my feet, vaguely aware of the tickling sensation of blood running down my arm and over my hand. "What do you mean she can't? She's my best friend!"

Willow leaned over Selina. Gripping Selina's wrists, she hit the hand with the knife against the grass over and over.

Selina screamed, and kicked, and bucked, but refused to let go.

The cut in my arm was smarting. "Selina, stop!" She had to settle down, or I might not be able to convince Willow not to hurt her.

My voice only made her wilder. With her eyes fixed on me, she thrust her hips, trying to buck Willow off.

When she stilled a moment to catch her breath, Jax ran forward and kicked the knife from her hand. It landed in the grass far from Selina's reach.

Fergus moved to stand between us, taking hold of my shoulders as I tried to step around him.

"Let go," I growled. "That's my best friend. Something's wrong with her. She needs my help."

Fergus squeezed my shoulders. I ducked away from his touch. I didn't think we were doing physical contact—he'd made that clear a few minutes ago.

"She's enchanted." His voice was soft, like he thought he was telling me something I might not want to know.

Or something I already knew.

I stilled. I hadn't known. But I should have.

Taking a breath to calm myself, I looked at her properly. Without panic filling my veins at her fighting like an animal against a fae she couldn't beat, I could see it. But only when I looked carefully.

Around the outside of her body, the air wavered, the same way it did above a road on a hot summer day. And mixed in with the wavering air were tiny flecks of red. My shoulders slumped. Even Selina wasn't safe. "Rhiannon?" Her magic was red.

Fergus nodded. "Looks that way."

"Can we un-enchant her?" Was that even a thing?

Fergus drew in a breath. "It's what Willow is trying to do now. She's had some experience with that. But there are some ... barriers." He stood shoulder to shoulder with me, watching Willow grow still as she held Selina's wrists against the ground.

"Because Rhiannon's so strong?" My voice wobbled. I couldn't let Selina live the rest of her life like this. She was like a wild animal.

Fergus shook his head. "Because we're in Iadrun. Not Faery. Our magic is weaker here."

Then the answer was simple. "Let's take her to Faery. It's not far, and..."

Selina screamed and bucked so hard she almost threw Willow off.

Fergus licked his lips. He was still speaking carefully. Still spelling out the things I should be able to see for myself. "How? We can't put her on a horse when she's like that and we can't carry her."

He had a point. Short of tying her up, which the way she was fighting probably wasn't possible, there was no way to get her there. I sighed. "So, what do we do?"

"Wait. Give Willow some time. We'll know if it's working soon."

I sank down on the grass and Fergus sat beside me. The silence between us stretched until it grew uncomfortable. We hadn't finished our conversation earlier, and I wasn't sure I ever wanted to finish it.

Jax watched Willow's every movement. "He looks like he's going to jump between Selina and Willow if things get bad."

"He is."

I dragged my eyes from Selina. I didn't like the way he said that. "It won't get that bad, will it?"

Fergus shrugged. "We'll know soon."

I was still angry and upset with what happened between us earlier, and so there was an accusation in my voice. "Why didn't you ask Willow to do this for Father?"

He shook his head. "I can't see a spell on your father." He frowned, twisting to look at me like he'd just thought to ask. "Can you see one?"

I shook my head. "No." But then, I hadn't seen the spell on Selina until he told me to look.

Fergus let out a deep breath. "I have no idea what's wrong with him. It's only a guess it's some sort of spell. With any luck, a few days in a space void of magic will be enough to suffocate whatever is affecting him and he'll be back to normal."

"Void of magic?" Lanwick had plenty of magic. Even I'd been able to use magic there.

"Where the Unseelie border meets Seelie, there's a thin strip of space where no magic exists. It's only a small space, most people crossing the border never notice it. But I have a vein of no-magic running through Iadrun. Sometimes, depending on the spell, going to a magicless zone can be the only option. It's just that the rest of the zone is above water, so it's only possible on my island. I hope it works for Myles."

A gust of wind blew across the yard, bringing with it the smell of something rotten. I pulled my cloak across my face against the smell and settled in to watch Willow.

Her magic reached out, a strand as thin as cotton writhing toward the faint magic around Selina's body. It hovered above Selina's chest, before darting amongst Rhiannon's magic. Beside me, Fergus' shoulders relaxed. I guessed the darting was a good thing.

Slowly, that little strand began releasing the flecks of Rhiannon's magic from Selina's body. Each piece she unhooked floated harmlessly into the sky, and with each piece that floated away, Selina struggled less.

"It's working, isn't it?" My shoulders relaxed. "Where did she learn to do that?"

"Many generations back, one of our family married a Dryad—a fae healer. Willow has inherited some of those healing skills."

"Like me," I whispered. Jax had called me a Dryad, too.

"Like you." Fergus' voice was soft. "A full Dryad only appears every ten generations. Between times, the healing magic is there, but weak. We had a full Dryad in our family five generations ago, so Willow's healing skills are about as weak as they come. But you, I'm guessing, haven't had one in your family for much longer than that, I'd guess nine or ten generations. As for where she learned how to do it, I believe some healing comes naturally."

"Like the way I knew to use the nightbalm berries?" And the blue mushrooms for Jax.

Fergus nodded.

"I need her to show me everything she knows." All I'd ever wanted to be was a healer, and here in Faery I'd done some amazing things while knowing virtually nothing. I could do so much more if Willow showed me how.

Fergus shook his head. "Willow probably can't show you much because she can't do much, but you're welcome to talk to her. There aren't many full Dryad's around, but if you want to learn from one, I can find someone to teach you."

I did. I wanted that more than anything. "Yes, please. As soon as we've sorted out Rhiannon, that is."

"Yes. After Rhiannon." We watched Willow in silence for a few minutes before Fergus spoke again. "Willow will remove as much as she can, but she doesn't have enough magic here in Iadrun to remove it all. It does look like she'll be able to do enough to settle Selina down."

I let out my breath. There was no way I was leaving Selina when she was like a rabid dog. "Is Rhiannon aware we're removing it?" In other words, should we be expecting her to turn up any moment?

"I imagine so." His tone was grim. "If she doesn't know right now, I'm sure she will know soon."

Selina's eyes met mine as I spoke with Fergus. "Bria?" Her voice was weak.

I got to my feet and approached her slowly. "Hi Selina. How are you?"

Willow sat crouched over Selina's waist, still pressing her hands against the earth.

Selina shook her head. "I don't know. Better. I think." She looked up at Willow leaning over her, and stifled a scream.

I crouched at her side. "It's okay, Selina. Willow's a friend. She's helping you."

Willow released Selina's hands and climbed off her. "I've done all I can for now."

Selina closed her eyes and drew in several long, deep breaths. "I honestly have no idea what's real and what isn't any more." A tear escaped the corner of her eye. She hadn't even tried to sit up.

I took her hand. "It's okay. This is real."

Jax stood guard, ready to jump on Selina should she attack again. I didn't think she would. She was already more like herself than she'd been a few minutes ago.

Selina blew out her breath. "This can't be real." Her laugh was hollow. "Because right now I think my parents are hanging from the living room ceiling, dead. And that the Unseelie Prince is standing over your shoulder looking like he'll kill me if I try to hurt you again."

She was wrong about Fergus—it wasn't her hurting me that Fergus was worried about, it was her hurting his sister. Hopefully she was wrong about her parents as well. I turned and glanced at Fergus. He nodded, already moving toward Selina's house, the sword from earlier appearing in his hand again.

I forced a smile. "Fergus is real. I'll introduce you once you're feeling better."

Selina's eyes drooped and her words slurred. It was as if by being here, I'd given her permission to relax. "He's even better looking than his pictures."

Fergus was still in earshot. I leaned toward Selina and whispered loudly, "He is. But you can't say things like that. He thinks too much of himself already."

She smiled and let her eyes fall shut.

Willow crouched on the other side of her and patted Selina's face. "Selina. You need to sit up. You can't sleep yet."

"I'm tired. Haven't slept properly in days." Her eyes remained closed, and a faint smile lingered on her lips.

Willow put a hand under Selina's shoulder and glanced at me. "Help me get her up. She can't sleep yet. We need to get her on her feet. If she sleeps, I can't save her."

I did as Willow asked, Selina's head lolling as she sat. "She'll die?"

Willow nodded. "If we can get her to have a drink of something, she won't feel as tired. Jax is getting water for her now."

I put Selina's arm around my shoulders, and Willow and I dragged her to her feet. "Selina?"

"Mmm."

"The prince is waiting to meet you. You need to open your eyes." If anything was going to get her to stay awake, it was that. She'd always had a thing for Fergus.

Willow raised her eyebrows at my lie. Fergus and Jax were currently out of view, inside Selina's cottage.

"And the Unseelie Princess is here, too. I need to introduce you to her properly, but I can't do that when your eyes are closed."

With much more effort than it should have taken, Selina forced her eyelids apart and turned her head to stare at Willow. "The Unseelie Princess is beautiful. But I don't like the way her fingernails dig into my wrists." Her words were slurred, each one sounding like it took an enormous effort to speak.

I glanced at Selina's wrist. Sure enough, there were four half-moon shapes gouged into her skin from where Willow held her tightly against the ground moments earlier.

"Sorry about that." Willow's voice was quiet.

"S'okay. Not every day a fae princess attacks you. Happy to have a war wound." She didn't even sound like herself.

Jax appeared from Selina's house, his face solemn. He carried a mug in his hand. "Here. This will help." He held the water to her lips and Selina drank like she hadn't seen water in a week.

I tried to catch his gaze, to find out if Selina's parents were waiting inside for her to return home, but Jax wouldn't meet my eyes.

When the water was gone, Selina let out a loud belch, then looked around the yard with clear eyes. "Bria? You're home?" She jerked when she saw Willow holding her up on her other side and Jax standing in front of her. She extracted herself from our grasp, wobbling on her feet before righting herself. "And you've brought fae with you?"

As if all previous conversations hadn't happened, I nodded. Selina caught sight of Fergus walking out of her cottage and burst into tears. "It's all true, isn't it?" She looked at him. "I hoped it was a dream, but you're here so it must be true."

Fergus walked up to her and nodded. "I'm sorry about your parents. But you're safe now."

I looked between Fergus and Selina. "They're … dead?"

Fergus nodded, but said nothing more.

I shook my head. They couldn't be dead. I'd known them most of my life. They were as constant as my own Mother. Selina looked stricken. I wrapped her in a hug which only made her cry harder.

Fergus' face was grim. His eyes met mine, and he spoke to the back of Selina's head. "I know you're upset, Selina. But can you tell us what happened?"

Selina pulled away and wiped her hands down her face. "It's my own fault. I've been so stupid." She shook her head and more tears ran down her cheeks. "I've been visiting Faery. A lot. To see Tobias' grave." She looked between Jax, Willow, and Fergus. "He was my baby brother. The Wild Hunt took him." Fergus knew that. As Xion, he'd shown Selina to Tobias' grave. "They must have seen me there."

"Seen you where? And who are *they?*" I rubbed a hand up and down her back, feeling useless to ease her pain.

"In Faery. I must have upset them while I was there, and two fae followed me home. I don't know who they were, but they appeared at the front door about a week ago, just after I got back. They started yelling. I tried to keep them out of the house because I didn't want Mother and Father to find out where I'd been." She shook her head. "But

I couldn't stop them. They stormed inside and tied Mother and Father upside down to the rafters and demanded I spy on you." She looked at me. "It wasn't much of a decision, I was checking your house every day anyway, hoping you'd come home. I said I'd do it and thought I'd gotten off easy."

Selina walked over to sit on one of the twin swings Father built for us when we were children. Her stare was distant. The rest of us followed, standing around her and waiting until she started speaking again. "I cut my parents down and for a few days, our lives continued as normal. I was starting to relax again, thinking they just wanted to scare me. But last night they returned. Told me they knew you'd been here and wanted to know what you'd taken with you when you left."

My heart dropped. We hadn't stopped here, but we had flown low over my house on the way from Willow's cottage to the Unseelie Castle. I looked between each of the others. "Rhiannon knew we flew past here." The idea she was tracking us so carefully made me ill.

Willow shrugged. She didn't seem to think it such a big deal. "A spell on your home using your own belongings as a base wouldn't be that hard to do." She put a hand on my shoulder. "Don't worry. There's no way she knows your other movements. The spell only told her you came here. Not where you'd been before that or where you were going."

"But it's probably telling her I'm here now."

She gave a nod. "That too."

Okay, so on top of everything else, we were definitely working to a time limit. We needed to hear what Selina had to say and get out of here before anyone arrived from Seelie.

Selina seemed to realize that at the same moment because she started talking again. "I told them I hadn't seen you, that I was certain you wouldn't have come home without visiting me, or that if you had, it must have been in the middle of the night and you couldn't wake me." Tears slipped down Selina's cheeks again. "They didn't believe me, and they were angry. It seemed like they were going to kill us all, so I pleaded for our lives, told them I'd try again. I'd do better. That..." She looked at her feet, her chest rising and falling as if she'd just run for her life. "...if you came back, I'd force you to stay until they returned." She shook her head and looked at me, her eyes pleading. "I didn't mean it. I'd never have handed you over to them."

I nodded. "I know."

Her voice turned hard. "Didn't matter, anyway. They wanted something else entirely.

They just needed me to agree to help. Once I offered, they stopped their yelling. I thought I'd saved our lives. I thought for once, I'd done something useful."

I closed my eyes. I could only imagine what was coming, and I didn't want to hear it. Crouching beside Selina, I put my hand on her knee. "You don't have to tell us, if you don't want to."

"I have to. I need to get it out of my head." She'd always been this way. If she did something wrong at school, or if something was bothering her, she found relief in speaking of it.

I nodded and stood. Fergus moved to stand behind me. He touched the small of my back with his fingertips, a silent message telling me we would get through this, that we'd all be all right. I didn't believe him, but I leaned back into him, willingly forgetting what had happened between us earlier. The physical touch gave me the strength to smile at Selina. "Whatever you need."

Selina blew out a deep breath. "All I did was dig a deeper hole for myself. And extended my own life by a day or two. They went after Mother and Father again. Father fought so hard this time. He was ready for them. After they left the first time, he placed daggers and two swords around our cottage, and he coated the entrances and windows in salt."

"Salt doesn't work," Willow and Jax murmured together.

Selina managed a weak smile. "Something I'm now aware of. However, yesterday my family expected it to help. When it didn't, Father dropped a bucket of nails over the head of one of them." The last word rose in pitch and she looked at Fergus.

He nodded. "Iron burns. A bucket of nails is a good defense."

Selina's eyes saddened, and she shook her head. "A good defense would have been one that worked. The nails only angered our attackers. The one that Father hurt took a few minutes to recover, then used just one hand to haul Father up, feet-first, and tie him from the rafters. That fae smirked as he cut Father's throat. While he did it, his friend held Mother and I in a headlock, forcing us to watch while the life—and the blood—drained from Father. We couldn't help him, and Mother couldn't take it. She started screaming and wouldn't stop. They slit her throat where she stood then strung her up."

"Oh, Selina. I'm so sorry." I should be crying, too. I'd known these people all my life. But no tears came. Instead there was white hot anger in my stomach and I might need to throw up at any minute. I didn't know how Selina was sitting so calmly as she spoke.

She continued through her tears as if she hadn't heard me. "They dragged me through all the blood on the floor to stand outside—just here, beside the oaks—and then, best as I can tell, they put a spell on me. That's where I stood ever since at their command. Through the pouring rain that came last night to the unrelenting heat today. I couldn't move to eat, to sleep, to check on Mother and Father. I thought I was going to die standing there." Her tears came faster, and she swatted them from her face with the heel of her hand. "Until I saw Bria walk into her cottage earlier. Then, suddenly, I could move. I found myself creeping around to the front window and watching you in the house. And the moment you took hold of the picture and put it in your pocket, the only thing I wanted was to rip it from you, then run into my house and hide."

I put a hand on her shoulder. "It's okay. You're safe now. You can come to Faery with us. Willow will remove the rest of the spell, and you'll feel more like yourself." I looked at Fergus, my mind racing off in a different direction. "I guess they assumed whatever I took from the cottage would be the intensifier." I shook my head. "They couldn't have got it more wrong."

Fergus looked like something sour sat in his mouth. "You know she can't stay in Faery with us. Not if she wants to keep her mind. I would have to spell her to keep that from happening." And then she wouldn't be herself.

Five hours. That's how long a human could last there. It was probably long enough to remove the rest of the spell, but then what? She'd return to her cottage, bury her parents and clean up her house while waiting for the fae to return and kill her because she didn't get what they'd asked her to? There was another option. "She's not human."

All three of my fae friends turned their attention to Selina's perfectly rounded human ears.

"Her great-great-great-grandmother—or something—was fae. She must still have some fae blood, right?"

Willow nodded. "Fae blood is fae blood."

"And she has been spending time in Faery, going to her brother's grave," Jax added.

Fergus nodded, his eyes thoughtful.

Before he could say anything, Willow decided for the rest of us. "Then she'll be perfectly fine." She held out her hand and helped Selina from her seat on the swing. "We have to leave. If we stay, those fae will return. Fergus has cut down your Father and buried both your parents already."

My gaze shot to Fergus. He had? As if I'd spoken out loud, Fergus met my eyes and nodded. The lightest sheen of magic surrounded him. I guess that was how he'd dealt with them so quickly.

Thank you, I mouthed.

As Willow led Selina to her horse and I turned to lock up my cottage, Jax came over to speak with Fergus. "I'm going to Unseelie." He whispered. Whether it was to stop me hearing or Willow, I wasn't sure. I turned back to listen. That sounded like a dangerous plan.

"What? Now?" Fergus shook his head, watching his sister.

"I should have thought of it sooner, but this—" He swept his arm around the yard and Selina's cottage. "This just proves how serious Rhiannon is and the lengths she'll go to get what she wants. If I check out what's happening there, the Hunt can rescue your father already knowing what they're up against."

"It's dangerous." Fergus spoke just as quietly. He wasn't worried about me hearing. It was Willow's ears they were hiding from.

Jax shook his head. "Not when you look like one of them."

Between blinks, his green hair changed to a mousy brown, and his clothes became the grey uniform of the Seelie guard. A shiny silver sword hung at his waist.

I took a step back. My head knew it was Jax standing beside Fergus but apparently my body didn't.

Jax laughed at my reaction. "I'll take that as a compliment." He stepped behind Fergus, hiding from Willow's gaze, but wasn't fast enough.

"Jax! What in the stars?" Willow rode her horse over to us with Selina nestled in front of her.

Jax whistled for Flame, who came trotting out of the forest. "I'll be back before you know it. It's safer this way." He didn't offer Willow any further explanation or wait for her complaints before jumping on his horse and heading into the forest toward the border.

Willow huffed and watched him leave. "Are you two ready?"

I nodded. "We'll lock up both cottages and be right behind you."

TEN

"BRIA!" Crystal came running across the large
grass paddock at Lanwick Island where the horses
lived. It was a wide and flat piece of land that
angled up from the beach to the base of the hill in
the center of the island. And it was always cool
here, spelled so the horses didn't have to put up
with the same heat the rest of us did. We'd just
arrived back from Unseelie, and Willow and I were
seeing to the horses, while Fergus helped Selina
into the house.

She beckoned with her hand.

My heart dropped to my knees. Crystal had
been looking after Father while we were gone.
Something must have happened to him.

"Go," Willow urged, taking Raven's reins.

I sprinted across the uneven paddock and down to where Crystal waited just inside the fence. When I reached her, she put up her hands, telling me to slow down. "Don't panic. It's nothing bad." She jumped the fence and waited while I climbed over after her.

"What is it?"

She smiled softly. "Myles is awake. And he's asking for you."

If she said more, I didn't hear. I broke into a run along the crushed shell path that led back to Fergus' home, not stopping until I knocked on the door of Father's room.

"Come in," he called.

My heart leapt. I might have been kidding myself, but it seemed he sounded better today than he had last night. I opened the door and poked my head around it.

Father sat in a leather chair, his feet propped up and covered with a blanket. He wore striped pajamas that I could only guess he'd borrowed from Fergus. He smiled when he saw me, the confusion in his eyes yesterday now gone. "Bria," he whispered, his voice filled with awe. "Come in."

"Father!" I ran to him and climbed into his lap, wrapping my arms around his neck. "I thought you were dead. If I'd known..."

He shook his head, a movement I felt rather than saw. "I'm glad you didn't. It was what the king wanted."

I pulled away. "The king did this to you?" Deep down, I'd known it. There was no other explanation.

Father sighed, his eyes roving over my face like he couldn't believe what he was seeing. The feeling was mutual. "He has an old quarrel with me because he once wanted to marry your Mother. He blames me for her not choosing him. More recently, he's wanted to ensure the potential bond you have with his son didn't form. He thought he could achieve that by leaving me as bait."

"Bait...?" I didn't understand. "You couldn't be bait if we didn't know you were there."

He looked away.

I moved into his line of sight. "I had no idea you were there, Father. I thought you were dead. I'd have come for you had I known."

He reached out and took my hand. "Which is why I'm glad you didn't know."

His sentence sounded unfinished. "Mother didn't know either." I couldn't quite make myself sound like I believed it. Which was crazy because she hadn't known.

Father licked his lips, refusing to meet my eyes.

"She didn't." She wouldn't have left him there for all these years. It wasn't possible. But then, not that long ago, I hadn't thought it possible she was a fae princess, either.

Father's gaze moved to the window. He said nothing, but he might as well have disagreed with me.

A sudden image of my first visit to Faery came to mind. The envelope with the ornate gold writing. The magic pointed tips that fitted perfectly to my ears. The way Mother tossed that envelope into the rubbish the moment it arrived each year. "You sent the invitation to the masquerade?"

Father nodded. "Your mother and Aengus wanted you and Prince Fergus kept apart. Neither of them wanted to tell either of you anything about each other, and all I could see happening was you getting hurt in their efforts to keep you apart. Or killed. I thought Prince Fergus, should you meet him, might stop that from happening."

I walked over to the window, then turned back to look at him. I wasn't dead yet. I wasn't sure if that was Fergus' doing or just dumb luck. "What did the king do to you? When we found you in the stables, you seemed like a different person."

Father drew in a deep breath. "Every year, the day after the masquerade, he forced me to drink a potion. It made me forget who I was, and I became who he wanted me to be, which was Milo, the stable hand. He used a potion because it was invisible to anyone who can see magic." He shrugged. "Invisible to Fergus."

I leaned back against the window frame. That made little sense. "How could you send the invitation if you didn't remember who you were?"

"By the end of each year, the potion wore off. I couldn't leave Unseelie, no matter how hard I tried, and I tried really hard—I needed the King's permission for that. But for a few days, I could remember who I used to be. The first year I sent a letter to Aoife, telling her where I was and what had happened. The second year, and every year after it, I invited you to the ball, hoping you and the prince might find a way out of the mess your parents have made for you." His eyelids drooped. He was still feeling the effects of the spell. "And it seems like you might have done just that."

I shook my head. There was so much to tell him. But not now. Not until the spell was totally out of his system. I pushed off the window frame and walked over to put a hand on his shoulder. "We have a lot to catch up on."

He smiled with his eyes closed. "And I have all the time in the world to listen."

I nodded. With any luck, I might soon have all the time in the world, too.

Once Father drifted off to sleep in his chair, I went in search of Selina. Fergus had given her a room beside mine. She lay on her bed as Willow worked on her, slowly removing the rest of the magic until she was certain she had it all. It was fascinating to watch. The queen's magic sank into Selina's body like barbed hooks, and Willow used her magic to straighten the hooks and pull them out. I was going to get her to teach me how to do it when we had more time.

Once she was finished and had left the room, I curled up on the bed beside Selina, not wanting to leave her alone. She'd lost so much in the past months.

Her eyes cracked, and she gave me a lazy smile. "So, you and the prince, huh?"

I shook my head. "It's not what you think."

"You mean the two of you can't keep your eyes off each other for some other reason than the bond that took you away from me and brought you to him?" Her eyes were closed as she talked. It wouldn't be long before she drifted off to sleep.

I wanted to tell her all the things that had happened these past months, but like with Father, it would have to wait. "We are bonded, but he doesn't feel anything for me."

Selina snorted. "Only a blind person would agree with you about that."

"Fine, then," I huffed. "I don't feel that way about him."

Her eyes opened, and she rolled over until she was lying on her side staring at me. I braced for her to offer some pearl of wisdom. Instead, she said, "If you say so."

My eyebrows rose, and I sat up. "What does that mean?"

"It means if you say all that back there in Iadrun—" She waved her hand around the room as if we weren't half a kingdom away from her home. "All the long looks and quick touches meant nothing, then I'll agree with you."

Long looks and quick touches? Fergus and I didn't do that. Except that I had leaned into his touch outside Selina's cottage. And I had spoken with my eyes, asking him to check on her parents. I shook my head. "Well ... it doesn't mean what you think it means."

Selina grinned. "I can't see what else it would mean."

I swallowed. Neither could I. "We're bonded, and it's the magic from our bond. It makes me do things I don't want to do." I pushed up off the bed, but Selina caught my hand.

Her voice was soft when she spoke, all teasing gone. "What's the problem? You seem happy around him." Her eyes narrowed. "Does he treat you bad?"

I shook my head. "No! Not at all."

Her eyes narrowed further. "And yet there's still a problem?"

I put my hand to my heart, then quickly let it drop when I recalled the way Fergus always did the same each time he reminded me of his title. "I want to *choose* who I fall in love with. I want it to be epic and real. I don't want it chosen for me. I don't want it to be out of my control."

Selina's eyes drooped. I should let her sleep, but I held my breath and waited to hear what she would say. I'd missed her so much these last months. I'd had no one to talk to about anything.

"Even if he's the best person in the entire world for you? Because, damn ... if I were you, I'd want to stare at him all day long." She spoke with her eyes closed, a wide smile on her lips.

"Even then." I didn't want something forced upon us by magic. I lay back down beside her. "He is nice to look at, but there should be more to a relationship than that."

"Girl, if I had someone stare at me the way that boy stares at you, I'd never go anywhere else again."

I awoke to the inaudible murmur of voices out beside the pool, and Selina's steady breathing at my side. For a few moments, I let the rise and fall of the voices wash over me, but curiosity won out, especially when I heard Jax's gentle laughter. He was safely back from Unseelie, then. The other voice belonged to Fergus.

I got up and crept out the sliding door that led to the pool, and into the heat of the island.

Jax and Fergus sat at a tall table, eating with their fingers from a platter of food, while Buttercup stretched out in the sun at Fergus' feet. My stomach rumbled—I couldn't remember the last time I'd eaten, but I was suddenly shy. Fergus and I hadn't spoken on the ride back here. We'd barely spoken since I thought I wanted to kiss him in the cottage, and things were awkward. I needed to apologize for wanting—for those few moments—the thing we'd agreed we didn't want. But I couldn't do it in front of Jax, and until I apologized, I couldn't make myself walk over to that table and act like everything was fine.

In the end, it didn't matter. Jax saw me hovering beside the door and beckoned me over. "Princess! Come eat with us."

I shook my head. Technically, the name he used was correct, but I wasn't and would never be a fae princess. I was raised human, and I still felt like one.

Fergus turned, his eyes falling on me and a smile pulling at his lips. He'd bathed and changed into casual clothes, and his shoulder length shaggy hair fell loose around his face. My heart stuttered in my chest. Not because of the way he looked. Because of the way he looked at me. Just like Selina said he did.

I tore my gaze away. Magic. That was all it was. I started toward them.

"Sleep well?" Fergus asked as I reached the table.

"Yes. Thank you." I'd slept better than I had in a long time. Perhaps because Father and Selina were safely here. Now, if only I could find Mother.

Jax's eyebrows lifted. My reply was overly formal. I hadn't intended to sound that way. I just wasn't sure how to act. I was so confused about everything. Jax looked between us, saw goodness-knew-what, and stood. "I have … something else to do."

I shook my head and stopped him with a hand on his arm. "Don't go on my account. I was hoping to hear what you'd found in Unseelie."

His eyes moved between Fergus and me, and he sank back into his seat. "I was just about to go over it with Ferg, but there's not much to tell."

"Oh, I highly doubt that." I took some bread from the platter, not bothering with butter before scarfing it down.

An amused smile formed on Fergus' lips. It suited him better than the frown he'd worn all the way back to Lanwick. "Hungry?"

"Starved," I said between mouthfuls. When I realized they were both watching me with grins on their faces, I put the bread down onto a napkin. "You were saying...?"

"No, no." Jax indicated to the platter. "Go ahead and eat. We've both just done the same thing."

I smiled and took another bite of bread. I was hungry. But I wanted to hear what he'd seen. "Are there still Seelie guards in Unseelie?"

"Hundreds."

I frowned. "You're kidding, right?" Because we didn't have hundreds of people at our disposal. Although I wasn't sure of exact numbers in the Wild Hunt, I knew it was less than one hundred.

"I wish." Jax sighed. "I don't think these are her best fighters, though, so that's something. It's like she's brought them as a show of power. Though this is only a fraction of her army if the guards I spoke to in Unseelie are to be believed."

"The Hunt could take some of them?" Fergus picked up an olive from the plate, rolling it in his fingers a moment before putting it in his mouth.

Jax nodded. "No problem. Most of the guards on the grounds weren't even carrying swords."

"Good." Fergus brought another olive to his mouth, his eyes distant and thoughtful.

I didn't understand why he was so glad about the sword thing. "But you don't carry a sword. Until you do." I'd seen a sword suddenly appear in his hand so many times these past few days that I'd almost lost count.

Amusement flashed in his eyes. He clearly wasn't holding a grudge about what happened in the cottage the way I seemed to be. "Must I continue to remind you?" He placed a hand on his chest. "Unseelie Prince. Very powerful magic."

A smile pulled at my lips. "And also, very full of yourself." His eyes caught mine and held. An offering. I smiled back. We were okay. Apologies could wait.

Jax cleared his throat. "Fergus has access to magic most of the rest of us don't." He shifted in

his seat and my cheeks heated for making him uncomfortable. "If Rhiannon's guards don't carry a
sword on their body, they most likely don't carry
one at all. They'll carry other weapons, like daggers or throwing stars, but Rhiannon prefers to
keep the odds tipped in her favor, and her sword-
wielders all have a certain magic, more akin to
yours and Fergus', making them more likely to
win in a battle against fae with less power."

"More akin...?"

Fergus lifted his palms. "They can form their
magic into a weapon that can shear right through
a person. Like me. And you."

And Jax, though he could only manage it a
single time. "She has multiple guards that can do
this?"

Jax nodded.

Well, that was frightening. "Do those without
swords also use their magic to fight?"

Jax nodded. "Sometimes. Though, mostly the
queen's frontline guard are hired thugs with more
brawn than magic."

I'd seen some of those thugs in the recent days.
"Naga?" A shiver ran down my spine as I recalled
their flicking tongues and beady eyes as they
poured poisoned salt into my mouth.

Jax nodded. "Along with many other types of
fae that have their own specific way of killing.

Keep your distance and you'll be fine, Princess."
He threw me a grin.

Fergus sat forward. "The Naga we met the
other day were typical of their type—they like to
work in groups. But not all her frontline guard
work that way. Some can render a person
immobile just by locking eyes with them. They
are dangerous in their own way, but the Wild
Hunt as a group are strong. Plus, we'll have the
advantage of surprise. We can kill most of the
guards on the grounds before they even realize
we're there." He looked at Jax. "What else did
you see?"

"Bodies. Lots of castle staff and servants dead,
their bodies scattered around the grounds where
they fell. And there's a huge concentration of
guards in the prison. Which makes me believe the
king is still there. I tried to get in, but short of
making a scene, it wasn't going to happen."

"Numbers?" asked Fergus.

Jax thought for a moment. "More than we
have, but at the prison, probably not many
more. It's doable, I think. Oh, and the queen is
there, too."

"The queen is at the castle? You're certain?"
Fergus asked.

Jax nodded. "She is searching for something. I
saw her as I passed Willow's rooms, but your

rooms are in the same messy state Bria's cottage was in, so I think she's been there as well."

Fergus frowned. "That makes little sense. We don't siphon off our kingdom's power to grow stronger like they do in Seelie. There's nothing in the whole of Unseelie that will help her in that quest."

Jax shrugged. "Well, she's looking for something."

"And you have no clue what she might be after?" Something about the way she'd turned Fergus' room upside down itched at my mind. She'd done the same to Willow's room. And to my house. But neither of those were the thing I was trying to recall.

"What do you think she's searching for?" Fergus' tone was careful.

I shook my head. "I don't know. But I feel like I should." I was missing something obvious.

"Could it be something your mother told you once?" Jax prodded. "Or your father?"

I shook my head. No. Whatever was bothering me had nothing to do with either of my parents. Most of the time, I couldn't believe I was here in Faery and not living with them in our cottage in Iadrun. There wasn't a single thing in my memories of them that would link them to Rhiannon. To think, I wouldn't even be here in

Faery talking about her had I not gone to the king's masquerade—

I slapped my hand onto the table. "The king's rooms!" That was it. The thing my mind wanted me to recall. "The day we disturbed her when she was glamoured to look like the king, Rhiannon was searching for something in the king's rooms."

Fergus shook his head. "I'm not sure how—"

"His sword, Hellfire." I nodded as I spoke, filling in the blanks in my mind. "That's what she was looking for, right?"

Fergus and Jax nodded.

"Many years ago, Mother was friends with him. What if she gave him that sword as a gift? A gift she wanted to hide in the least likely place possible."

Fergus frowned. "She didn't, but to follow your thinking through, why would she? And why would the queen care?"

Jax shook his finger at me, following my line of reasoning. "Because it was actually her intensifier. Also known as the Royal Sword."

Fergus shook his head. "Nice theory, but Hellfire has been in our family for centuries." His face soured. "Had, I guess. Since she took it with her that day."

My shoulders slumped. For a moment, I was certain I'd figured it all out. "There's no chance you could be wrong?"

"Sorry. But I could show you plenty of old texts and paintings around the castle of relatives carrying that sword." He stood to leave. "I should speak with the Hunt about tonight."

I nodded. There was no point sitting around in the sun when there was work to be done. "I'm coming to Unseelie when you go."

Fergus licked his lips. "It's going to be dangerous and we haven't had time to work on your magic..."

I knew all that. But I wasn't sitting around waiting here for them to return. Or not. "Then you'd better hope it works as well as it did with the naga today." Fergus grinned, gave me a nod and started back toward the house.

Jax got up and followed him, speaking over his shoulder. "Be ready to leave at six."

I watched them go, the two of them laughing with each other as they wandered away. When they were almost at the door into the house, I jumped up so fast, my chair tumbled backward, clattering against the pavers and making Buttercup spring to her feet. When she saw it was just me being clumsy, she moved to a shady spot beneath the table, turned in a circle and lay down again. Fergus and Jax both turned to stare at me. "Your naming ceremony!" I pointed at Fergus. "You should have received a sword that night."

Fergus' nod was slow, and he took a step toward me.

"And didn't you tell me once that it wasn't an heirloom?"

He nodded again, his eyes lighting. "Father was given it by an old friend. I always thought he was giving it to me because he didn't care for it and didn't know what else to do with it. He said Mother would have wanted me to have it."

"What if the old friend that gave it to him was my mother?" It would certainly make sense for Indira to want Fergus to have something that belonged to her oldest friend.

Jax nodded. "If the queen knew she was searching for a sword but not which one, it would answer why she was looking in your father's rooms. She probably thought his sword was the one she needed."

Fergus walked over and picked up my chair. "And when she realized it wasn't, she returned and searched my rooms. And Willow's."

"Would she have found your naming ceremony sword in any of those places?" That was really all that mattered. If she'd found it already, there was nothing we could do. But if she hadn't, perhaps we could beat her to it and stop her ridiculous quest for greater power.

Fergus shook his head. "No. Father keeps a selection of swords in his rooms, as you know. If it had been there, the queen would have taken it already and stopped searching."

I waited for him to say something else. When he didn't, I gave him a push. "So, where would it be?"

He shook his head. "I'm trying to think..."

"Would Willow know?" Jax asked.

"Would Willow know what?" Freshly bathed, and with her hair pushed up beneath a hat to keep the sun from her face, Willow walked out of the main lounge to where we stood beside the pool.

Fergus glanced her way. "Where Father would hide things. At the castle."

Willow tapped her fingertips against her lips, thinking. "What kind of things?"

"The sword for my naming ceremony. Or possibly something else Aoife Ridgewing might have given to him or Mother."

Willow thought a moment, then her eyes brightened. "What about the cavity beneath the bed in Mother's rooms?"

Fergus frowned. "Her rooms have been closed up since she died."

"And yet you know there's a cavity beneath her bed." Willow grinned. She looked at me. "He pretends to never put a foot wrong, but when he was feeling brave as a kid, he used to sneak into Mother's room through the tunnel passage and play in there. If Father had caught him..." She shook her head. "I doubt he'd still be alive."

Fergus pursed his lips. "And you know this because you were right there beside me, every step of the way."

Willow laughed. "That's true."

Fergus nodded. "It's a good hiding place."

It was an excellent suggestion. A sword Mother gave Indira hidden in Indira's rooms. It was possibly the perfect hiding place. "We should check it out while we're at the castle." I looked between Jax and Fergus. "Or, I could go alone, if you need to stay with the Hunt." I lifted my eyebrows. "At least you won't need to worry how my magic behaves if I'm not near the fighting."

Riding with the Wild Hunt made me want to whoop and giggle. I'd loved flying with Raven since the very first moment I climbed on her back, but I suddenly understood at least part of what made Fergus desperate to hold on to this part of his life.

Ahead of me, visible only by moonlight, as far as the eye could see, were mask-clad fae, riding on the backs of horses of black, grey, chestnut and white. At the horse's feet ran the hounds, Buttercup included, who barked almost as hard as they ran. There was no formation. Horses dipped and weaved. Some circled back to run beside a friend, others raced to take the lead. Every one of them wore a mask, and their hair and cloaks flew out behind them on the wind. "I had no idea there were so many of you in the Wild Hunt." There were far more than one hundred people riding tonight. Many horses carried more than one person.

Fergus rode beside me. Or should I say, Xion rode beside me. His masked face was serious, and there was a furrow between his eyebrows. I wondered when I'd stopped seeing that wide-mouthed skeleton as scary. Somehow, even as Xion, he still looked like Fergus to me. He seemed uninclined to whoop and holler, which was about the only thing I wanted to do. "Some of them are my people. Most of them are their families. Everyone wanted to help rescue the king from Rhiannon."

"They chose a dangerous time to offer assistance." I was under no illusion about how tonight might go, and I hoped they weren't either. People would die. I just hoped there wouldn't be too many of our people who didn't come home. I shook my head, surprised at how far I'd come these past months. Not long ago, all fae were my enemy. Now I was thinking of the Wild Hunt as my people.

"They thought it a worthwhile cause." Fergus nodded at the empty sky over my shoulder. "Go on. Take this chance to ride like you want to."

"I already am." It was a lie, and Fergus knew it.

He shook his head. "I know the way it calls, the night sky. Go. Enjoy it."

It did call. I could think of nothing better than having Raven run as fast as she could, dipping and weaving, while my hair snapped around my face. "Come with me?"

Fergus shook his head, the crease between his eyebrows growing.

"Then I'll pass." I wanted to go, but I wanted to go with him. It could wait. With any luck, we'd have another chance to run the horses like the wind sometime soon. "What's wrong, Fergus?"

He shook his head and sighed. "No matter how I look at it, I can't see a good outcome from to-night."

I knew what he meant. He wanted to rescue his father, but at the same time, his life would be easier if he didn't. We hoped to find out something about my mother, but there was a chance she had teamed up with Rhiannon and was working against Fergus and me. "Beating the queen to the intensifier will be a good outcome." At least, it would if none of the millions of things that could go wrong came to fruition.

Fergus nodded. He looked as convinced as I felt.

I stood at the edge of the forest at the southern end of the castle, waiting for the Wild Hunt to storm the prison. They would wait until Fergus cleared the grounds then, led by Jax and Crystal, would begin their attack and hopefully free the king. Much to Fergus' concern, Willow was with them.

I wanted to join them, but until I figured out how to use my magic, I was a liability. I was just as likely to kill one of our own as someone on Rhiannon's side, and I wasn't risking that.

Fergus didn't even say goodbye before flying Obsidian from the shelter of the forest to drop down inside the castle walls. For a moment, I lost sight of him, my vantage point on a rocky outcrop not quite high enough to see over the walls. Then the glow of his magic appeared in the darkness, a deeper blue now than it used to be. He moved fast, stopping for mere seconds before moving on. It was eerily quiet and I couldn't see what he was doing, but I knew. Each time he stopped, he killed. No one fought back, they didn't know he was there or hear him coming. He was quick, and he was lethal. It was the least fair fight I'd ever seen, but it was the only answer to this huge army that had invaded his home.

He returned, panting, his magic barely glowing around his body, and removed his mask, stuffing it into a pocket in his black pants. He looked no less grim without it on.

"Did it go all right?"

He nodded. "I've evened up the numbers to give the Wild Hunt a chance. Now they just need to find Father and rescue him." He directed me back through the forest. It was dark and my eyes had barely adjusted when he found the tunnel and pushed me through the entrance I didn't see until we were walking through it. He'd only completed half his job tonight.

We walked in silence, our feet light on the packed earth. My heart raced, and I wrapped my arms around myself against the cold as we started up a set of stairs. This was it. The other half of what we'd come here to do tonight. Although it should be simple from here, I couldn't shake the unease that hardened my gut.

We reached the door to Indira's rooms and Fergus pressed his ear to it, listening. When he heard nothing, his magic flared. He unlatched the lock and pushed the door open.

Indira Blackwood's rooms looked like she could walk in at any moment. The bed was made and topped with so many cushions of turquoise, white and blue that it was almost impossible to see the bed. The fire was set, and as I ran my fingers over the dresser, not a mote of dust came away on them. I'd bet there were still clothes hanging in her closet. It was no wonder her young children had enjoyed playing in here so much. It must have seemed like their mother was still alive when they came into her rooms.

We tiptoed across the thick rug covering the floor, Fergus carrying a small ball of light in one hand—something else I'd have to get him to teach me how to do the moment we had time. He nodded to the bed and got down on the floor, pointing beneath it to where I needed to search at the head of the bed. This was why I was here. I was small enough to get under the bed without moving it, something Fergus definitely couldn't do.

On my stomach, I crept forward, chin to the ground. There was little room beneath the bed, as expected. I put a hand out in front of me, working from touch in the long shadows cast by Fergus' light. I was looking for a ridge in the floorboards, something so minute it couldn't be seen, only felt. When I located it, I wedged the knife I held in my other hand beneath it and pried it open with my breath held.

I desperately wanted to be right about this sword. And even more desperately wanted to get to it before Rhiannon found it. With the floorboard out of the way, I placed my hand in the dark hole. I closed my eyes, hoping I would not find a dead rat in here.

Or a live one.

But like the rest of Indira's rooms, the cavity beneath the floor was meticulous. No dirt. No dust. Nothing.

And not a thing inside it.

With rushed sweeps, I ran my hand around the cavity again. It had to be here. We didn't have a Plan B. We barely had a Plan A.

My hand brushed something in the back corner and my breath caught. I shuffled forward to reach it better.

Cold metal. A carved handle with a curved pommel.

A sword.

Hopefully, *the* sword.

With a smile, I wrapped my fingers around it pulled it from the hiding place. I froze when it banged on the wooden floor as I brought it out, but no one came running into her room, so I replaced the floorboard and backed out.

"Well?" whispered Fergus. I held up the sword. He broke into a grin. "Outstanding work." He nodded to the tunnel door. "Let's get out of here."

As we crossed the room, the door to Indira's rooms crashed open, and light flowed over us.

Fergus clutched my arm and dragged me toward the tunnel, but my feet wouldn't move.

Because standing on the threshold of Indira's rooms was Queen Rhiannon.

ELEVEN

RED LIGHT filled the room, and magic dragged my hands behind my back. I struggled against the force holding them, the sword still dangling from my fingertips. But I couldn't free myself.

Fergus' hands were behind his back, too. A thick band of red magic held them in place.

"Well, well. What have we here? An unexpected surprise." Queen Rhiannon looked over her shoulder and beckoned, and four guards filed through the door behind her. "It appears to be my lucky day." Her deep burgundy dress rustled as she moved, and her heels tapped on the wooden floor. Her long hair was piled elaborately atop her head and shining jewels nestled between the strands.

The guards moved to stand in front of the open cupboard door that was the entrance to the tunnels, while two more appeared, waiting outside the door Rhiannon had strolled through.

"Actually, I lie," laughed Rhiannon. "I was expecting you. And it's turned out even better than I imagined. You seem to have found the very thing I've been searching for." Her eyes dropped to the sword hanging from my hand behind my back before lifting again to fall on my ears, her nose wrinkling in disgust.

I couldn't pull my hair over my ears with my hands behind clamped my back, but I didn't want to. Rhiannon's disgust at the way I looked was her problem, not mine. I lifted my chin and stared straight back at her.

Fergus' magic pooled around him, the deep blue fighting against Rhiannon's red magic to light the room.

Rhiannon blinked at him, her voice turning hard. "Don't do anything stupid, boy. You know you're no match for me."

That was what she thought. She might have beaten him before, when he'd barely cared to fight. Now he was stronger.

And together, we were stronger, again.

I called on my magic, letting it form around me. We could beat her if we worked together. We could end this here and now.

Her eyes moved to me and she looked me up and down. "That would also be very unwise, niece."

"I disagree." I spoke through my teeth, concentrating on calling up my magic.

Until I understood the reason she'd bound our hands.

If we couldn't use our hands, we couldn't point our magic where we wanted it to go. There was nothing either of us could do against her while she held us like this.

Still, Fergus' magic grew around him. Perhaps he knew something I didn't.

Rhiannon must have thought so, too. Moving slowly, she brought one of her hands up to hip height. She beckoned with her fingers to something just outside the door. A smirk formed on her lips as Mother walked in and stopped like a shield between Rhiannon and Fergus.

Mother was dressed like she was going to a ball—or like she was a faery queen—in a red dress with a sparkling bodice and A-line skirt that split right up to her thigh. Her golden shoes had toothpick heels, and she wore her deep brown hair piled on her head like Rhiannon, with a crown atop it all.

"M-mother?" I glanced at Fergus. "Please don't hurt Mother!"

But I didn't need to ask. His magic had already burned away, though he watched Mother and Rhiannon through narrowed eyes.

Mother looked at me, her gaze as hard as Rhiannon's. "I expected better from you, Bria. Fighting on the side of the Unseelie." Disgust dripped from her voice.

I shook my head. The woman I'd grown up with didn't speak to me this way, not ever. And the one time she'd met Fergus and Willow, she'd treated them with respect, not contempt. I looked at Rhiannon over Mother's shoulder. "What have you done to her? What spell have you used to get her to work with you?" I would get Willow to show me how to remove it rather than leave Mother this way, even if it took the rest of my life.

Rhiannon laughed like I'd told the funniest joke. "I didn't need a spell, child. Ask your mate. I believe he sees magic. He can tell you she isn't enchanted."

But I didn't need Fergus to tell me. Rhiannon didn't know, but I could see it myself. And no matter how hard I stared, there was nothing on her body like the spell Willow had pulled from Selina. There was no magic on her body at all. I glanced at Fergus in case I was missing something.

He shook his head. He couldn't see a spell, either. "A potion, then. You've used something hidden."

Mother shook her head. "I've taken no potion. I'm here of my own accord."

Rhiannon shrugged. "Aoife is family. She knows where her loyalties lie." There was a needle in her voice, a pointed dig at me.

"Is that the same loyalty you showed me by dragging me beneath your castle and placing me in a cell to die?" Because of that and many other things, this woman would never earn my loyalty or trust. I couldn't think what she might have said to bring Mother to her side.

Rhiannon shrugged. "You understand, I had to make sure you were really who you said you were." Her gaze dropped to Mother standing in front of her. "Shall we move on?"

Mother cast a disgusted eye around the room. She didn't seem to care that she was standing in the place her best friend had once slept. A room that seemed to look exactly as it had when Mother knew Indira. "Gladly." She walked over to me, so much taller than I was used to seeing her in those shoes. "Goodbye, daughter."

I shook my head. "You don't have to go with her."

Mother kept walking, closer by the second, and I suddenly realized why. This was all an act.

Without Rhiannon's watchful eye on her face, Mother was going to give me a sign that she needed help. Or she'd free our bonds. She'd never go near a woman as cruel as Rhiannon unless she was forced. Eyes on mine, she smiled. It was good to see her smile, I'd wondered if I would again. She put her arms out to hug me. I stepped into them, waiting for the comfort they would bring, listening for whatever she was about to tell me.

But she wasn't there for comfort.

She was there for the sword.

She ripped it from my hand.

I didn't even see her move. One moment her hands were out wide, enclosing around my body, the next she'd yanked the sword from my fingers and had it gripped between two hands, a maniacal grin on her face.

I launched at her, hands still tied. There was no way I was letting her give that to Rhiannon.

But she moved fast. Too fast for me to reach her. Too fast in those ridiculously high shoes.

Rhiannon laughed again. I was getting mighty sick of that sound. "Oh dear. It appears you are too slow and the thing you came searching for has fallen into the hands of your enemy." She looked at Fergus as she spoke, each word a barb.

Her glance reminded me of all the scars on Fergus' back from her suppressors. Some of them were from before I'd known him, but he held many scars she'd caused recently.

My magic grew around me. I hated that woman. Hated her for what she'd done to Fergus. And for whatever she was doing to Mother.

Fergus moved closer to me. I understood what he meant—he was warning me to be careful, not to do anything stupid while we were trapped in a small room with all the exits guarded. But I didn't want to be careful. I wanted to get rid of that woman who stood in front of us, taunting me.

As she turned on her heel, I pulled on my hands until my magic pushed the bonds apart. Then I thought about my magic hitting the center of Rhiannon's back. I imagined it burning a hole into her burgundy dress, her staggering then dropping to the ground. I thought about the way my magic so often shot out in a different direction and told myself it would not happen this time. Then I let it go.

At the last second, I saw the glimmer of a shield around Mother and Rhiannon. But it didn't matter, anyway. My magic did what my magic always did, and shot out the side of my hand, skimming past Fergus' face to bury deep into the wall over his shoulder. Dust and stonework toppled to the ground.

Mother was already out the door, standing off to one side and waiting for her sister. Rhiannon gazed at me, an eyebrow raised. "Oh, dear child. It would seem spending time with the enemy is not at all good for you. Your magic appears to be broken." Another laugh, and she swept out the door.

As Mother passed the doorway to follow her sister down the corridor, she glanced at me, her eyes demanding. She touched her fingers to her hair.

Then she, too, was gone.

I started after her, but Fergus caught my hand and held me back, the bonds on his hands disappearing with the queen. "Don't. They're shielded. We can't stop them."

I pulled away. "We can. Together. The same as we did with your father at your naming ceremony."

He shook his head, his eyes sad. "We can't do that again. Bria, I—"

Running footsteps in the corridor outside Indira's rooms stopped him speaking. His magic grew around his body. But it was Jax who skidded to a halt outside the door. Willow followed closely behind.

"You're okay," Jax puffed, bending over and resting his hands on his knees.

"As are you," Fergus said carefully. He pulled his shoulders back. "Father...?"

Willow stepped into the room, her eyes falling on the bed, then the dresser, making me wonder how long it had been since she'd visited this place. "He's fine. Rhiannon was holding him in the prison as we expected. But he's free now. Heading to the throne room and he wants to see you."

Fergus ignored her last comment. "The Seelie?"

Jax shrugged. "Gone. The ones you didn't kill, at least."

"Gone?" How could that be? There were so many of them here just minutes ago.

Jax nodded. "We were winning, cutting down guard after guard as we moved closer to the center of the prison. We were almost there—I could hear your father calling for help. Then there was a flash of red and all the uninjured Seelie disappeared from the prison. Must have realized they couldn't win and ran back to where they came from."

I hoped that was true, but something told me they hadn't left because they thought they were losing. They'd gone because Rhiannon thought they'd already won.

Willow looked between Fergus and me. "Did you get it?"

I shook my head, tears welling in my eyes until I could not speak. Mother was my enemy. And I'd failed everyone else in the worst way, practically begging her to take the sword from my hands.

"We were set up." Fergus dropped down to sit on the edge of his mother's bed, letting his head fall into his hands. "Rhiannon knew we were coming. She expected me and Bria to find the sword. She was waiting, and she took it from us. Now she has what she came for and she no longer has any use of this castle—"

"Or us as prisoners," I added. Though I wasn't certain why she kept taking Fergus prisoner, she no longer needed me. The only reason she'd ever needed me was for my intensifier. The way she'd demanded Mother take the sword from my hands was enough to confirm it was Mother's intensifier, now in Rhiannon's hands. She either already had mine, expected Mother would tell her where to find it, or only needed one of them to become the most powerful fae in the realm. Either way, Rhiannon was now an immensely powerful woman. Or Mother was. I guessed we'd have to wait to see on that count.

"Or that," Fergus agreed. "Now she's gone, and the castle is ours again. She's taken all her people. Probably back to Seelie, where I can't even think about what her plans might be."

If only we'd moved faster, got out of this room the moment I had the sword in my hand. If only we'd kept it away from them. "We had it. They took it from my hands." I should have fought harder to hold on to it. I hadn't fought at all. Mother had simply slipped it from my fingers. "I'm sorry."

"You couldn't have done anything more than you did." Fergus got to his feet. "No point sticking around here. Let's go."

"Father wants to see you." Willow spoke like she didn't want to, repeating the words Fergus had ignored earlier.

Fergus' face was hard as he crossed the room to the tunnel. "Father can wait."

Willow shook her head. "You know he can't."

I could see on Fergus' face he knew exactly that. And also that there was very little he wanted to do less than visit his father right now. I slipped my hand into his. "We can go together."

He looked down at our joined hands and blew out a laugh. "I fear that would be the very worst thing we could do."

I pulled my hand from his and stepped away. He was right. The king didn't want Fergus to have anything to do with me, even if we were just friends.

He shrugged and met my eyes. "But, if I have to go to him, then the only way I want to do so is with you by my side." He glanced at Jax. "What of the Hunt?"

"Some injuries. No deaths. Crystal is organizing them. Some are already on their way home."

Fergus nodded, starting out of the room. "Good."

We heard the king before we reached the throne room. His voice filled the air with what seemed like a never-ending rant. Unseelie fae rushed past us in both directions, their faces harried, some still injured and bleeding from the fight with the Seelie.

I stepped into the room at Fergus' side. Although smaller than Rhiannon's throne room, it was no less grand. Midnight blue carpet led from the entrance where we stood all the way across the room and up four steps at the opposite end. Tapestries of deep blue and gold hung from the walls. And seated on a throne at the top of the stairs was the king.

He yelled orders at a group of fae when we entered. Fergus didn't wait for the king to call us forward, taking my hand and walking along the carpet to where his father sat. Willow and Jax followed a step behind.

"Fergus." Disgust rolled from the king's tongue. "So glad you could finally join us."

"Good to see you, too, Father." Fergus' smile was forced. As were his words.

"Of course, it's typical you would arrive now, once the hard work is done."

Fergus swallowed and bit his tongue while I silently urged him to tell his father he had been here the entire time, that it was because of him that the grounds were clear enough to get to the prison in the first place. But he said none of that, and I doubted it mattered, anyway. King Aengus would believe what he wanted about his son.

The king's gaze fell on someone at the back of the room. "Get me Xion Starguard!" There was a shuffling of feet as that person left the throne room.

Willow stepped up to the dais. "I believe Xion sustained an injury in the battle, your Highness."

"Is he alive?" the king growled.

She paused before answering. "He is."

"Then he will come to me as I command."

Willow inclined her head. "As you wish."

I didn't dare look at Fergus. There was no way Xion could make an appearance in this room at this moment. Not while Fergus was here, too. And for Jax to help, he'd have to leave without causing a scene. Tension thrummed through Fergus' hand, but his posture remained relaxed. Which was opposite to the way I felt.

With a messenger dispatched to bring Xion in, the king's attention turned back to Fergus. "Even your sister played a part in sending those psychopathic Seelie fae back where they belong. But not you." He shook his head. "I should be beyond feeling disappointed in my only heir, but what a surprise. I'm not."

Fergus tensed and I squeezed his hand. I was here for him, however he decided to handle this. His chin jutted. "Yes, Father. That's what I'll always be, your biggest disappointment. Now, was there a reason you called me in here, other than to voice your displeasure in me after all these months apart? Because I've got places to be." The words rolled from his tongue like he was bored, a tone I'd never heard from Fergus before.

The king's gaze moved to me. "No doubt you prefer to be locked up in your rooms with your new mate."

Fergus tensed as if he was about to spring at the king. I gripped his hand tighter. I knew bullies, and that was what Fergus' father was. The king wanted a reaction. Better to give him nothing. Fergus blew out a breath, the tension leaving him.

There was movement behind us, and the king looked over our heads. "You're not Xion Starguard."

Footsteps sounded. "Xion is injured and regrets he cannot meet with you tonight. He said he will come to you the moment he's seen a healer. In the meantime, I am here to do his bidding." The voice was a hollow monotone in the same way as Fergus' voice once he put on a mask, but this one wasn't so deep. I was fairly sure it was Crystal. Thank the stars she hadn't left yet.

The king nodded. "I don't suppose it matters so long as I have someone to do my bidding."

Fergus tensed. I ran my thumb across the side of his hand, sending thoughts I wished he could hear; *let it go, it doesn't matter, we'll be done here soon.*

"What do you require, your Highness?" Crystal asked.

"Get your people to find all the Seelie left on my grounds and throw them in the prison. Starting with this one." He pointed his thumb in my direction.

Fergus stepped in front of me. "If you take her, you must take me first."

The king stared at him for a long moment. "Don't tempt me, boy." He nodded at Crystal, telling her to do as he asked. But Fergus stood so Crystal couldn't get near me. Not that she was trying. "You won't be marrying her, Fergus. You might as well accept that now."

"I don't plan to marry her—"

"Good!" The king's voice echoed around the room. "Then she can go to the prison. Where she belongs. It's where I should have put her the last time I captured her."

"No!" Fergus roared. "I won't let you treat her this way. She's a good person. She's good for me. You will not lock her up in a cell tonight. Or any night, for that matter."

The king got to his feet, looking down on us from his dais, his nostrils flaring. "You would prefer I kill her? Because that remains an option high on my list of favorites."

Fergus shook his head, his lips curling with disgust. "I'm not doing this. Not tonight. Or ever." He turned, grabbing my hand.

The king's magic flared, midnight blue, the same color as his décor, and quicker than I could move, a bolt of magic flew toward us. He had taken no time at all to call it up.

I put my hands up in front of me, as if that would help stop the blast. A pink sheen of magic formed around Fergus and me.

A shield.

I'd made a shield!

In the same instant, Fergus' shield appeared, meeting and joining with mine within the space of a heartbeat. The king's magic hit hard, but not hard enough to damage us.

The same couldn't be said for the king, though. His magic bounced off our shield, flying straight back at him to bury into his thigh. He stumbled and fell, his screaming curses the only sound in the room. Blood flowed from his gaping wound, but it didn't flow as fast as it should, nor was there as much blood as I expected from such a wound.

Fergus squeezed my hand, pointing at his father with the other. "Whatever happens now, Father, remember you wanted it this way." He took a step back, still glaring at his father.

"Boy! Get back here. Can't you see I'm injured!" The king clutched his leg, pain creasing his face.

Fergus lifted his chin. "I see it. I just don't care."

"Willow!" the king bellowed. "Daughter, come save your father's life."

Willow stood between her brother and her father, looking at each while they waited for her to choose. She was in a horrible situation, I wouldn't want to make the decision the king was forcing upon her.

Fergus saw it too. "It's your choice, Willow. I won't hold it against you, whatever you decide."

He pulled me back another step. I couldn't get out of here fast enough.

Willow shook her head and followed us.

"Daughter! I'm dying!"

Willow whipped around to face him, anger making her voice harsh. "You are not dying. You were hit by your own magic, and you know as well as I do that your own magic can't kill you. It might take some time to heal, but perhaps you can spend your recuperation thinking about how badly you've treated my brother all these years." She stalked past us. "Come on, Ferg. Let's get out of here."

"Daughter!"

We turned our backs on the king and walked out. At the door, Fergus stopped, taking a last look back at his father. "In case you haven't worked it out yet, you don't command the Wild Hunt any longer. I do. And I'm taking them with me." He took out his mask and placed it over his face, showing his father who Xion really was, and just how much power he actually had.

I could still hear the king bellowing as I climbed on Raven's back and started for Lanwick.

TWELVE

I SAT WITH my feet in the pool, the chilled bite of the water a relief from the humidity in the air. The sun was rising, a deep orange color flooded the sky and cast a strange light over the island while the waves made their relentless yet hypnotizing attack of the beach.

"Want to hang out here for a year or two and sit out what's coming?" Fergus lowered himself down beside me, kicking off his boots then pulling up his pants to put his feet in the water.

I smiled, but it wasn't the cheerful kind. "Tempting." But unlikely. "I thought you were in bed."

"Why? Thinking of joining me?" His comment had the desired effect, an unchecked grin coming to my face. I punched his arm. "That's more like it." He watched my smile. It made my heart race.

I thought everyone else was in bed. There were no lights on in the house, and I'd left Fergus and Willow alone hours ago to come to terms together with the stand they'd just made against their father. I didn't bother trying to sleep. There was too much going on in my mind for that to happen, no matter how tired I was.

Fergus sighed. "I was in my room, about to climb into bed, and I looked out my window. There was a beautiful lady sitting down by the pool, and I just had to come down and sit with her."

I smiled into my chest. There was no doubt Fergus Blackwood knew how to give a compliment. It must have been all those years at court, complimenting the pretty fae women that surrounded him. "You just missed her." I nodded toward the beach. "I think she went that way."

He grinned. "She did nothing of the sort. She didn't want to pull her feet from the cool water."

That was true. My feet didn't feel like going anywhere right now.

"I was serious before. You can stay here as long as you like."

"Thank you." I knew that. "But it's not practical."

"Neither is war, and there's one coming." There was no lightness left in his voice.

I nodded. I knew that, too.

"Rhiannon's very powerful, and I fear we've made an enemy of her."

We had. But it wasn't a reason to cower. "We're powerful, too, you know. The two of us. Together."

He stared at me for a long moment. "Have you changed your mind? About our bond?" His voice was quiet.

I shook my head. He'd been perfectly clear about his feelings, and even if I sometimes had trouble sorting my feelings from the ones the bond made, I would never force something on him he didn't want.

He nodded. "Then there's something else you need to know." He licked his lips. "It's about our bond and I probably should have told you sooner. I just didn't think it would matter because it seemed like we wouldn't be spending much time together." He shook his head. "Seems I was wrong about that."

"Do you wish we hadn't spent so much time to-gether?" Because I enjoyed being around him. Lately, it was one of the few enjoyable things in life.

That smile that pulled at my heart formed on his lips. "Never. But it creates another small ... issue."

I lifted my eyebrows.

"Each time we join our magic, it's like telling the bond we accept it, and so the bond grows stronger ... it's magic digs deeper into us. I have found someone who thinks they can release us from it, but it will be painful." He lifted a shoulder. "Worse, because we've joined our magic twice now. Plus, there was that kiss..."

The one that had caused the bond to start.

"That sort of physical contact has the same result."

He'd found a way out of this. "So, no more joining magic or kissing at naming ceremonies, and we could be free of this thing?" Stars. Why did it hurt so much to say that? I didn't even want the bond, so I shouldn't feel like my heart was shattering just saying those words. The sooner I was rid of this magic controlling me, the better. "When can your person perform this spell that will unlink us? Because I'm ready now." I got up, but Fergus pulled me back down beside him.

His hand remained loose around my wrist and I did nothing to pull away. "We get one chance to remove the bulk of it, but we can never be completely rid of it."

I frowned. "I don't understand."

"I can get someone to take almost every part of our bond. It will mean the feelings we sometimes have for each other will disappear and everything we feel will be our own again. But that thread will always be there, and if we join our magic after we've had the bond removed, our bond will grow again, and it will be there for good."

No more feelings for Fergus Blackwood. I could deal with that. I could. "So, you're saying we should wait until after the war?"

Fergus nodded. "If you plan on returning to Iadrun once we've stopped Rhiannon..." He pitched his words like a question.

I nodded. All I wanted was my old life back, the one where I was a human healer, not a fae princess.

He swallowed, looking past me a moment before he spoke again. "If that's your plan, once the war is over, we won't need to see each other again and there will be no chance of our magic joining."

Never see each other again. I straightened my spine. I could deal with that. It was exactly what I wanted. "You're saying we have one last thing to do, then it's back to life as we know it?"

He looked out to sea. "I guess that is what I'm saying."

Fergus grew quiet after that and left not long after. As light filtered across the world, I thought about Mother. Father was going to be disappointed when I told him where she was and what she was doing. I still didn't understand why she had teamed up with her sister and what was in it for her.

The way she'd stared at me as she passed the door, though. It was like she wanted to speak to me, even if she'd made that all but impossible by wearing Rhiannon's clothes, her hairstyle, her princess crown.

Mother had touched her hair as she stared at me.

I pulled on my loose locks at the bottom of my neck, running my hands through the strands and dragging them away from my face.

Oh.

She *had* been telling me something.

I jumped to my feet.

"Fergus!"

With that one gesture, Mother had told me everything I needed to know about my intensifier. Better still, she'd as good as told me they were still searching for it.

Maybe there wouldn't be a war after all. Maybe we could stop it.

All we had to do was find my missing hair clip.

Because that hair clip was my intensifier.

And it was wrapped up in an old pile of clothing that I'd left somewhere in Rhiannon's castle.

To be continued in book three of the Royals of Faery series:
Kingdom of Tomorrow's Truth (available for pre-order now)

———

Already missing Bria? For a different type of kick-butt heroine, try Maryanne in the Sherwood Outlaws series.

This is a complete series, available for purchase or free in Kindle Unlimited on Amazon.

———

Reviews are an important way for authors to find new readers, and finding them means we can pay our bills a little longer! I'd love it if you would take a few minutes and leave a review for this novel—it doesn't have to be long.

———

GET THE ROYALS OF FAERY PREQUEL NOVELLA FOR FREE

Thanks for reading Kingdom of Today's Deceit.

If you're not quite ready to leave Faery yet, sign up to my reader list and I'll send you Kingdom of Times Forgotten for FREE! You'll also get a copy of Outcast, the prequel for my Sherwood Outlaws series, also free.

Just use the link below, then complete your email address.

I look forward to meeting you.

https://www.hayleyosborn.com/times-forgotten/

ALSO BY HAYLEY OSBORN

ROYALS OF FAERY
Kingdom of Times Forgotten (prequel)
Kingdom of Yesterday's Lies
Kingdom of Tomorrow's Truth

SHERWOOD OUTLAWS
Outcast (prequel)
Outlawed
Outplayed
Outlasted

About the Author

Hayley Osborn lives in Christchurch, New Zealand, with her husband and three children, cat and dog.

Online, you can find her at:

www.hayleyosborn.com.

To connect with her on social media, you can find her on Facebook at HayleyOsbornAuthor, on Instagram at Hayley_Osborn_Author or on Twitter at @Hayley___Osborn. Or if you prefer to make contact via email, you can contact her at hayley@hayleyosborn.com.